SERGEANT CLUFF
LAUGHS LAST

Detective-Sergeant Cluff is at home in the bleak, moorland market town of 1960s Gunnarshaw. A gruff and gloomy loner, he has spent a lifetime observing local folk – and knows their lives inside out. They know him, too – a bulky, macintoshed figure who watches from the shadows of Gunnarshaw's ginnels as they go about their daily business, his dog Clive always at his side.

But it's not just criminals Cluff has to watch out for. Never satisfied with easy answers to cases, Cluff is a maverick and no flatterer to authority – much to the bemusement of Detective-Constable Barker, but much more so to the despair of the hapless Inspector Mole, who tries at every opportunity to outwit or contain Cluff's singular methods of detection.

But beneath Cluff's dour exterior beats the heart of a truly compassionate man who possesses a deep understanding of human nature, in all its sordid and depraved details – details which frequently push Cluff to bend the rules in his pursuit of moral justice.

Gil North's novels, which follow the investigations of Detective-Sergeant Cluff in the fictional and close-knit moorland market town of Gunnarshaw, were first published in the 1960s. Incredibly popular, they were adapted for BBC Television and regularly attracted twelve million viewers. Gil North wrote the scripts for every episode.

Gil North was the pen-name of Geoffrey Horne (1916–1988). He was born in Skipton, North Yorkshire, where his father was Town Clerk. Horne was educated at the local grammar school, then studied at Christ's College, Cambridge, before embarking on a career as a civil servant in Nigeria and Cameroon.

He later returned to pursue his writing ambitions in his native Skipton, which was not only the inspiration for Gunnarshaw, but also the location where the television drama *Cluff* was filmed.

SERGEANT CLUFF LAUGHS LAST

Gil North

GREAT NORTHERN

This edition published 2021 by
Great Northern Books
PO Box 1380, Bradford,
West Yorkshire, BD5 5FB

www.greatnorthernbooks.co.uk

Originally published in 1964 by Chapman & Hall Ltd

ISBN: 978-1-912101-39-9

Design by David Burrill

CIP Data
A catalogue for this book is available from the British Library

CHAPTER I

"You'll live through it," Annie Croft said. "There's worse things at sea."

"I ought to be certified."

Annie grinned: "It's the penalty of fame."

The Sergeant glared at her: "I can get myself ready."

"Someone," Annie told him calmly, "has to see you don't give them the slip. I wouldn't put it past you."

Clive sat on his haunches, velvet-soft eyes lifted to his master's face, troubled by this departure from routine. Even the cat in the seat of Cluff's armchair wore a faint expression of astonishment.

He buttoned his waistcoat and arranged the chain of his half-hunter across the swelling of his belly. His hands trembled very slightly and the stiff edge of his well-starched collar bit into his neck. He ran a finger inside it and the day wasn't that warm but he could feel a thin film of sweat on his forehead.

She held out his jacket and he thrust his arms into the sleeves, more uncomfortable than ever as she settled it on his shoulders. She stood back and ran an appraising glance over him. His Sunday-best boots shone like glass: the neat, dark-blue suit clung to his big frame, perhaps a little too closely, a tightness under the armpits, the cuffs of the trousers a shade too high, revealing more than they should have done of matching blue socks clocked with grey. He demanded, angrily, "Will I do?"

Annie adjusted the knot of his tie and renewed her inspection. She stretched out her arm and plucked an infinitesimal piece of fluff from a lapel: "It's the best we can make of you."

He pulled out his watch and compared it with the clock on the mantel and put it back in his waistcoat pocket again. The dog continued to gaze at him sympathetically: Jenet, in the chair, abandoned any attempt at a solution of this problem, curling tighter into a ball of fur and hiding her eyes with a paw. "Time won't go any faster for you watching it," Annie remarked.

"I could have walked."

"A fine state you'd have arrived in."

"What did they pick on me for?"

"I've been wondering."

"He's late."

"Stop worrying. He'll get you there."

"It's all right for him: he's only got to sit back and laugh."

They heard a car drive up the lane outside the cottage and stop. "Here he is," Annie said, handing him his overcoat, a heavy, camphor-perfumed garment with a belt, and ran a brush lightly round the crown of his rusty bowler hat: "You're not going to a funeral."

Inspector Mole entered the room importantly, very neat in a lounge suit, his cheeks scrubbed, shaved to perfection, not a hair on his head out of place. "Ready?" he asked heartily, eliciting a jaundiced look from the Sergeant.

"It should have been you," Cluff said.

"Not at all!" but the denial came too pat, and a tinge of envy, or of disappointment, coloured the Inspector's tone.

"Don't let him out of your sight," Annie warned. "I've had to watch him like a hawk all morning."

"We'll hold on to him: I've got Barker as reinforcements."

"It's a marvel," Cluff commented bitterly, "you didn't bring the Chief Superintendent as well."

"He's there waiting. Didn't you know?"

"Who told him?" the Sergeant said before Annie pushed him into the passage to avoid a quarrel. "My notes?" he exclaimed, with a trace of panic.

"Keep calm!" and she put them into his hand. She shut the living-room door to keep Clive inside and stood in the porch, watching them down the path to the gate, shaking her head. Detective-Constable Barker sat in the back seat of the Inspector's minicar, preened and polished too, but his smile faded under the impact of the Sergeant's frown.

The Inspector chauffeured with his usual care, making the couple of miles to Gunnarshaw seem endless, and so far as Cluff could see the dashboard block had developed a severe case of over-activity. He got hotter under the collar and he couldn't decide which of the two he favoured most, Mole's caution or the racing clock that brought the hour of his torment closer.

They turned between stone gateposts carved with a heraldic device and traversed an all too short drive ending in a wide macadamed space that flanked a conglomeration of buildings walled mostly with glass, fronting fields dotted with white goal-posts and patterned by the white lines of playing areas. A sonorous hum emanated from the assembly hall of the school.

Barker held his hat while he eased himself awkwardly from the car and it wasn't as bad as it could have been but it was bad enough. The waiting headmaster said, "Sergeant," and at least they didn't wear gowns and mortar boards here but the children were still children in spite of having failed their eleven-plus, a bit more frightening, perhaps, because of it. Cluff managed, "Mr Rigsby," in reply and followed like a criminal an executioner, guarded by Mole and Barker, to a staff room. There wasn't so much as a cup of tea in sight let alone the stronger stimulant of which he felt so much in need.

He allowed them to divest him of his bowler and overcoat and he wasn't himself without his stick and his tweeds and his dog. Rigsby whispered, "They've turned up for you in force," as they came through curtains on to a platform and Cluff's fingers rustled the pages of his speech. He wished he'd never accepted this invitation, foolish pride his downfall.

Row after row of faces floated in his vision, Chief Superintendent Patterson from C.I.D. Headquarters in the middle of the front line of chairs below him, honourably placed in the company of the headmaster's wife and their daughter, Janet, a gaggle of mothers and an occasional father stretching back to the middle of the hall, a herd of pupils behind them, girls on one side of the central aisle, boys on the other. Mole and Barker came in through a side entrance to seats reserved for them and who was the architect of his misfortune?

A double half circle of teachers and school managers, farther back on the platform, enclosed him and from what the headmaster was saying no one would have believed the

Sergeant had ever had a wrong word with any of them. The Chairman of the Managers flanked him on one side of the table, Rigsby on the other and, though he tried to slide down out of view behind the barrier of books stacked in front of him, it wasn't high enough. He heard the headmaster say, "We at Gunnarshaw Secondary Modern School—" and lost the thread of what followed but it came easily and without interruption, Rigsby not merely practised in speaking but aware of his oratorical skill. The Sergeant, attempting to divert his mind from his approaching ordeal, thought the headmaster too self-confident, too assured, too self-important, spurious because, after all, he wasn't Gunnarshaw born and the few years of his stay in the town hardly entitled him to such forthrightness about it and its inhabitants. Out of the corner of his eye he watched Rigsby, athletically built, probably a sportsman in his past, smiling and nodding, taking credit for the achievements of the school in the last twelve months, by no means glossing over his own contribution.

The grin on Patterson's face was peculiarly inane and Rigsby had vacated his pulpit in favour of the Chairman, a Gunnarshaw worthy for whom the Sergeant had no great love. He heard, "Not only have we here as our guest this afternoon a local man known to each and every one of us but a man who, by the nature of his work and the brilliance with which he performs it, has placed the community in his debt, a man dedicated, selfless and devoted to his duty—" The speaker paused for effect, intoxicated with verbosity, smiling at the outburst of applause, and the Sergeant, who would have welcomed it if the floor had opened to swallow him, scowled more blackly. "Who can forget?" the voice droned on, "the courage with which this friend of ours, only a few weeks ago and at such serious cost to himself, faced a madman who, but for him, might have thrown hundreds of us out of work and undermined the very economic structure of our community?"*

His cheeks flamed: he didn't know which way to look: he could feel the sweat trickling from his jowls. Rigsby nudged him to his feet and Lodge, the deputy headmaster, recited a list of names between each one of which a boy or a girl thrust a hand into the Sergeant's, receiving in return a book from those piled on the table. He opened and closed his mouth, hoping that the words were appropriate, and suddenly he was isolated, his notes crumpled in his fist, surrounded by a silence in which he could have heard a pin drop. The faces staring up at him came into focus and there wasn't a single one he didn't know, none of them that hadn't passed him in the High Street as he stood with Clive at his favourite post, letting the world go by. They didn't want a speech and he wasn't going to give them one. He crushed his notes into a ball and started to talk, as he would have done to any of them he'd met individually, the only difference that they couldn't answer back. He spoke about Gunnarshaw and his boyhood in the town, his birth a few miles away at Cluff's Head farm, about the countryside, his deep satisfaction to be one of them, and his contentment with his environment. Even the children, already restive from an excess of verbal gymnastics, quietened and hung on his words.

*   *The Blindness of Sergeant Cluff*

CHAPTER II

He was back in his chair, with the Chairman of the Managers whispering in his ear, "If you stood for Parliament you'd get in on a landslide," and he didn't believe it, because while he was one of them he was apart and who knew but that tomorrow or the next day he'd be faced again with the inevitable conflict between duty and friendship? He tried to remember what he'd actually said but he couldn't and he had the impression that now it was over the audience wanted nothing more than to disperse as quickly as possible. The senior boy voiced a vote of thanks seconded by the senior girl and Rigsby brought this part of the proceedings to a close, his eyes straying to a woman, not young but chic and well-preserved, who was leaving the rank of teachers for a piano in the corner of the platform. He said something about tea in the dining-hall and about exhibitions of handicrafts in the Woodwork room, of drawing in the Art room, and then they all sang the National Anthem, which surprised Cluff because he'd believed patriotism a neglected virtue, but gratified him as well.

They took him down the steps into the body of the hall not back through the door at the rear of the platform. People nodded to him and murmured, "Caleb," and he nodded back, a little drunk with relief. "Well done," Patterson congratulated him, and Mole smiled and Barker looked very cheerful. "My wife," Rigsby said, and the Sergeant put his hand out, though the woman was no stranger.

"Ruth!" the headmaster exclaimed, more sharply, his wife preoccupied in a world of her own, her eyes fixed on a point over Cluff's shoulder. He half turned his own head and caught a brief movement of Rigsby's in the same direction, to where the teacher who'd accompanied the anthem was closing the piano.

"She plays well," Cluff said, but the headmaster replied, "My daughter—" and the Sergeant asked the girl beside him, "You're not working today?" something beyond his own nervousness, from which he was rapidly recovering, spoiling the occasion now that he felt ready to enjoy it. Did he imagine these surreptitious glances, implicit with private meaning, the mother at the father, the daughter at both of them, this perceptible awkwardness with each other they strove to overcome?

The woman from the piano approached them: "Mrs. Fairchild," and Rigsby laughed. "But you're all friends. I'm the intruder. How long will it be before I'm recognized as even a probationary resident of Gunnarshaw?"

"A lifetime," Lodge, who'd followed them down from the platform, interrupted.

"Another of the natives," and the headmaster turned to Patterson, "My number one."

"We're old acquaintances," the Chief Superintendent told him. "I was born in Gunnarshaw too."

"I'm forgetting."

"Alone?" Lodge said to Mrs Fairchild. "Your husband isn't

here?" and she answered, "He couldn't get off." All at once the Sergeant felt islanded, the group silent, its members suddenly at odds, the policemen, Patterson and Cluff, with Mole and Barker hovering on the outskirts: the teachers, Rigsby, Lodge and Mrs Fairchild: the neutrals, Mrs Rigsby and Janet, or had they a foot, these two, in both camps?

"But tea," the headmaster proposed, and they followed him dutifully.

Cluff sat at a small table with Rigsby and his wife and the Chairman of the school managers. Men and women kept coming up to him, interrupting the trend of his thoughts. It wasn't Rigsby's fault if he'd been remotely concerned in the Culter case, that had ended with the incident at the mill mentioned by the Chairman from the platform, his discovery of Todd's body, its presence in his garden, fortuitous. The Sergeant knew he ought to be wary of his judgments after the mistake he'd made about Culter and hadn't he learnt his lesson yet? But the headmaster talked too much, in himself everything of which his guest had a constitutional dislike, a public figure moving in spheres far wider than that of his school, a finger in too many pies – dramatic societies, discussion groups, Library and Road Safety committees – making himself heard, scorning a position in the rank and file, a self-appointed leader laying down the rules and formulating the policies, standing no nonsense from the less educated. His job, no doubt, predisposed him to the exercise of authority, over adults as well as over children, but Cluff mistrusted this carry-over into his non-professional life and had little time either for those who tolerated it or for its principal.

The tables accommodated only four people each. To one side of the headmaster's Patterson and Mole took tea with Lodge and Mrs Fairchild, on the other Barker and Janet Rigsby shared their meal with a couple of Gunnarshaw educationalists. The canteen staff moved in and out from the kitchen, with teapots and plates of cakes, serving parents determined to get as much of something for nothing as they could: a buzz of conversation mingled with a smacking of lips, with the champing of imperfectly-fitting false teeth and the rattle of spoons: the prouder mothers of the prize-winners commiserated hypocritically with those whose offspring had failed to attain such dizzy heights of scholarship.

The Sergeant's increasing prejudices depressed him. From time to time he caught something of the polite conversation between Mrs Fairchild and Patterson and she attracted him no more than Rigsby did, though something in the Superintendent's manner indicated that he wasn't alone in his attitude. It irked him that as a married woman she found it necessary to go out to work, that she'd no children of her own to add to the total of those she taught. He couldn't understand why Mrs Rigsby's gaze wandered continually to the teacher and moved sharply away at the first hint of her interest being noted. The headmaster's studious unconcern with this particular member of his staff seemed too careful to be genuine.

The Sergeant said, "Yes", or "No", at intervals, at that no quieter and no more loquacious than the headmaster's wife, unapologetic for his own silence but worried by hers, which all the same might have been characteristic and probably was. A number of years of marriage sufficient to produce the girl of seventeen giving so little encouragement to Barker's efforts at sociability could hardly have left the mother unaffected, whatever of spontaneity she'd possessed in her youth.

He didn't like it: he couldn't find much he did like: it shouldn't have been like this. He'd got the speech over that had been troubling him for days, without, unless the townspeople had been extraordinarily kind and over-subtle in concealment of their real reaction, making too great a fool of himself. He'd done his part as a public figure for the first time in his life and he'd no intention of ever being inveigled into a repetition but his exultation and his relief were too short-lived. He ought to be sitting back relaxed, basking in the general approval, not striving to account for the way that woman with Patterson affected him and the others. He couldn't recall any rumour about her or any scandal in which she had been implicated and no one else thought it strange she'd returned to teaching after so long a lapse of time. If he believed that woman's place was the home others had more progressive ideas and admired her rather than condemned her for answering a call to public duty. She'd nothing to tie her to her house, unless a husband mattered, and why waste the training she'd had when she was young?

Patterson listened to her, Barker stared at her, but Janet Rigsby's eyes were riveted on her father. Lodge, the deputy head, leaned back in his chair, a half triumphant, half sneering expression on his middle-aged, moustached face, an untidy man whose domestic misfortunes excused, to some extent, his appearance. Mrs Rigsby fidgeted and Inspector Mole, left out of the conversation between Patterson and Mrs Fairchild, looked not only uncomfortable but annoyed.

She wasn't strikingly beautiful, she wasn't young, in her mid-thirties perhaps. A comparison between her and Mrs Rigsby, the one ten years older than the other, probably equally pretty a decade ago, by no means ugly now, had no validity. The headmaster's wife, to the naked eye at any rate, had kept her figure too and she had no grey in her dark hair. Until recently, whenever he'd seen her, the Sergeant had credited her with a calmness and a placidity that must have been comforting to live with – too comforting, perhaps, if carried to excess, boring. He shook himself mentally, disgusted with this creation of mountains out of molehills, and warned himself again to stick to facts, to leave people alone. There weren't any facts and, if there were, they didn't concern him.

The food had been eaten and the teapots drained, strength ebbed by the speeches recruited to undertake the tour of the school Rigsby suggested. Apart from an odd parent or two lacking faith in the ability of their progeny to produce anything worthy of inspection only Rigsby's table and its two neighbours remained occupied. The Chairman of the Managers showed signs either of impatience or of wanting to go to a lavatory.

Had the incidence of their relationships changed? A moment ago Janet's eyes, as she gazed at her father, had reminded Cluff of those of a whipped dog but now, as they rested on Mrs Fairchild, they blazed with hate. The triumph in Lodge's face had been transferred to the teacher's as she glanced at Mrs Rigsby. The deputy headmaster had forgotten them all except Janet, at whom he stared as if her clothes were no bar to his vision. The minds of the headmaster and his wife met briefly and parted without coming together again.

They didn't take Rigsby up when he repeated his invitation to the classrooms. The Chairman, making excuses, left and Mole said something about having to get back home: Cluff, who never lied, told one now and deceived nobody: Patterson pleaded the forty miles drive back to County Headquarters: Barker, clearly, had no intention of being marooned on his own in an environment closer to him in time than to the others.

Lodge and Mrs Fairchild wandered out, perhaps to superintend the crowds in the corridors, and Rigsby didn't press them to stay. The Sergeant refused an escort to the outer door and led his party away, very conscious of the family – father, mother, daughter – he left behind.

They reached the parking lot and, "I'll take you back," the Inspector offered, making for his own vehicle in the line of cars.

"Don't bother," the Chief Superintendent told him. "I'll run Caleb over myself."

"I thought you were in a hurry."

"Only to get out of there."

"It's no trouble to me," Mole objected, suspiciously.

"Nor to me either, Inspector," Patterson replied. He waited until the red minicar had driven away before he opened the doors of his saloon and glanced at the other cars: "Whose are they?"

"The staff's mostly," Cluff answered, and pointed to a popular model: "Hers."

Patterson remarked, without asking for positive identification of the Sergeant's reference, "She doesn't strike me as the sort who'd do much walking."

"She can afford one," Cluff said. "She's working, and so is her husband."

"As what?"

"A clerk."

"It doesn't sound much."

"She probably makes twice his wages."

"Awkward," the Superintendent suggested. "It wouldn't do for me. Or for you – you'd want to be master in your own house."

"His," and the Sergeant indicated a black Austin belonging to Rigsby. He motioned to Barker to get into Patterson's car and climbed in after him.

Clive ran out as Annie opened the cottage door for them, jumping up at Cluff. "Watch your clothes," she ordered. "They're your best."

"I shan't want them again in a hurry," the Sergeant replied.

"You made a muck of it then?"

"On the contrary," Patterson interrupted, "he spoke like a politician."

"Is that what's wrong? It hasn't improved his temper."

"No one asked you to stay on," Cluff told his cleaning woman.

"I won't, not when I've got you lot fed."

"Not for me," the Superintendent refused.

"And what did they give you at that place?"

"Perhaps you're right."

The Sergeant left his bowler and overcoat in the passage and removed his jacket in the living-room, unbuttoning his waistcoat and loosening his collar-stud, pulling the knot of his tie down to his chest. Patterson picked Jenet up and stood with his back to the fire, fondling the cat. Barker sat quietly on the couch.

"It wasn't pleasant," Patterson said.

"What wasn't?"

"I don't know what – emotional undercurrents, the whole atmosphere—" and he stopped, aware that Annie had returned to the room with tureens and a roast.

"Another of you," she commented, and eyed her employer. "Leave that sort of thing to him, Dan Patterson, and he's one too many."

They settled with their feet under the table and after Annie had gone back to the kitchen Cluff said, "Mrs Fairchild had plenty to say to you."

"I'm a married man," Patterson answered.

"She's a married woman."

"That's what I meant."

"That girl—" Barker began, but the Superintendent's presence awed him.

"What about her?" the Sergeant asked.

"She never spoke. She didn't seem to hear when I did."

"You're not her type," Cluff said.

Patterson interrupted, "She's got a boy?"

"Not that I've seen or heard of."

"She should have. She's old enough."

"I'm not going to tell her so."

"She's attractive."

They both looked at Barker, who bent his head over his plate and ate for a while before he qualified Patterson's judgment, "To look at."

"It isn't everything," the Superintendent concurred.

"There's something missing."

"Even in Gunnarshaw," and Patterson threw a glance at Cluff, "you get all sorts."

The Sergeant said, "There's nothing against the Rigsbys. I'd have known about it. They live a normal life."

"When you last heard."

Cluff's face darkened.

"It depends," the Superintendent added, "what you mean by, normal. Different people have different standards. Who, for instance, endorses yours?"

"Not many people these days."

"That woman – Mrs Fairchild – amongst them, I'd think. On the other hand, you might feel something in common with Rigsby's wife."

"Didn't you come to hear me making a speech?"

"It's your division," Patterson said, as Annie returned with clean plates and removed the dirty ones. Halfway through the pudding she poked her head round the door again: "The kettle's on the boil and the tea's in the pot. There's three of you to do the washing-up."

"I knew there was a catch in it," Patterson joked, but, later, he was the first of the three men to leave, avoiding any further reference to the afternoon except that he said, "I'll be hearing from you, Caleb."

"If I've anything to say."

After he'd gone Barker sat on the couch watching the smoke drift lazily from Cluff's pipe, putting a hand down now and then to Clive's head. The cat slept on the Sergeant's knees and they didn't talk any more but he wasn't offended when he finally set off through the moonlight on his way to Gunnarshaw. It had happened before and he'd have stayed longer, all night if need be, had the Sergeant not come to himself and sent him off.

His feet rang on the pavements of the deserted High Street and the clock in the church tower struck half past eleven before he was halfway along it. He smelt tobacco on the breath of the uniformed constable who stepped out of a doorway and demanded, "What's up?"

"What would be up?" Barker answered question with question.

"Been courting then?"

"Maybe."

"It's about time you suffered like the rest of us."

"You don't look to take much harm."

"It's the mental strain. Wait till you've lived with a woman."

"I'm taking a leaf out of Cluff's book."

The constable laughed: "He's worse off than any of us. He's got Annie Croft on his back."

"He can sack her if he wants to."

"By gum, I'd like to hear you say that to her face."

"I'll sleep sound," Barker said, "with Gunnarshaw in your hands."

"I wouldn't say the same for the Inspector. He knows me a bit better than that," the constable retorted.

He had to pass the police station on his way to his lodgings. The blind covered its window and its door was shut but presumably a light burnt in the outer office. He almost went in, more than half convinced he might just as well be on the spot as called out in the middle of the night, but he wasn't absolutely sure of the presentiment he had and he was afraid, if nothing happened, of looking foolish.

Although he went to bed when he got home he didn't sleep but lay awake, watching the track of the moonlight through the window move across the floor, his ears pricked for the ringing of the telephone in the hall of the house at the bottom of the stairs. The first time his eyes closed he dreamed that he heard it and he had the clothes thrown back and his legs out of bed before he realized his mistake. The moonlight faded and the room grew black and then the dark, in its turn, began to pale.

He would have bet a fortune that Sergeant Cluff missed nothing of the dawn either.

CHAPTER III

The light shone into Barker's eyes, stimulating a dull ache in his head. He opened them and it wasn't true. His limbs felt heavy and his tongue unpleasantly furred.

He hadn't been able to sleep and he couldn't have slept but what was he doing here with the sun streaming through the window whose curtains he'd left undrawn? He stretched out a hand for the watch on the bedside table and for a long time he couldn't take in the position of its fingers.

He leapt out of bed and dressed himself without stopping to shave. "Mr Barker," his landlady called, coming out of the kitchen door, releasing a savoury smell of frying bacon, as he dashed downstairs, and he shouted back, "I'll get something to eat in the town," grabbing his hat and coat from the hallstand.

In the street he set off almost at a run, startling a dog with its leg cocked against a wall, causing the eyebrows of a woman he met and nearly knocked over to rise in surprise, but he slowed before he got to the police station and asked himself, "What the devil am I rushing for?" The bright morning light and the unchanged appearance of Gunnarshaw suddenly underlined the absurdity of his actions. The night, like so many others, had passed without incident: no one had rung him up on the telephone to demand his presence: Sergeant Cluff, if he'd risen from his bed, was probably still at the cottage.

He stopped to adjust his collar and tie and to fasten the
buttons he'd missed in his haste. He straightened his hat on
his head, shrugging the set of his coat more comfortably on
his shoulders, a fair man whose whiskers weren't too obvious,
and stooped to knot his shoe laces properly. He argued with
himself whether or not to go back for his breakfast and finally
abandoned the idea because he could think of no satisfactory
explanation if he did.

In spite of himself he began to hurry again. His cheeks were
red, his armpits damp, and he was panting for breath when
he entered the station, with a haste that caused the Duty
Constable to lift his head with a jerk. The clock on the wall
told him it was earlier than he'd thought and both the door
of the C.I.D. room and that of Mole's office across the mouth
of the corridor leading to the back of the station were firmly
closed. Nothing had altered in the outer office, its atmosphere
normally somnolent, the customary silence unbroken, the
Duty Constable as usual leaning on the counter, a part of the
furnishings.

He took his hat off to wipe his forehead with his hand and
shook himself like a dog just out of water before he slid the
Complaints Book on the counter round to face him. The lines
on the page headed with today's date swam in his vision, the
page white and virgin, and he blinked. "Something on fire?"
the Duty Constable asked.

"The Sergeant?"

"He'll not have recovered from yesterday."

"Nothing?" Barker said, pushing the book away. "Nothing
at all?" knowing that his question merited no reply. He felt
empty, drained, let down, disappointed – he didn't know

how he felt – but the excitement still bubbled. The Duty Constable's lethargy and the familiarity of his surroundings failed to quieten his expectation. He wanted whatever had to come to come quickly so that he could deal with it and have it over and done with.

The newspaper the constable was reading rustled as he made his way back to the street door, unable to remain long in one place. The clarity of the spring morning sharpened every detail of the town's physical appearance and the red coachwork of the Inspector's car sparkled as it drove up to stop by the kerb. He left the station door open and fled before Mole could wriggle out of his seat.

He rounded the corner at the bottom of the High Street as the church clock at its top began to strike a quarter to nine. Schoolboys and girls in a variety of uniforms, blazers with badges, caps sewn in different colours, hats with brilliant bands, satchels slung from their shoulders or carrying little suitcases in their hands, swam against a stream of office-workers and shop assistants. The horns of buses and lorries blared at the pedestrian crossing. Neatly dressed men with briefcases got out of cars they'd this minute parked on the setts between pavement and carriageway and made for the entrances to banks and professional chambers. An ordinary day, entirely and completely ordinary, the only strange feature this first breath of spring, this lack of greyness, this softening of the town's grim, habitual mood. The people moved spryly: a note of gaiety sounded in the voices he heard, an optimism spawned by the sun and the blue in the sky: tiny buttons, delicately, shyly green, peeped on the branches of the ornamental trees planted along the length of the street.

A dissociation burdened him, a sense of apartness. He didn't belong and his coat contrasted with the blouses and the sports jackets. His unshaven cheeks made him feel dirty and neglectful, uncouth, a tramp of a man, an outcast, and his stomach rumbled for food, magnifying the hopelessness in his heart.

He moved only because movement was less conspicuous than standing still, avoiding the brooms sweeping dust from the shop entrances, halting now and again to allow the passage in front of him of men carrying armfuls of cartons from wholesalers' delivery vans. Blood dripped from the muzzle of a hare which a fruiterer and game merchant lifted on the end of a long pole to join a line of its companions suspended from gleaming chromium hooks over a wide, unshuttered window. The owners of stalls busied themselves stacking their wares for public display and propped handwritten price cards against the mounds they made of their goods.

He walked with his head bent, his mind filled with a foreboding foreign to the morning, his spirits depressed instead of elevated by the weather. He became aware only gradually of the broad back clothed in the stained Burberry swaying ahead of him, of the sharp, regular tap of the stout walking-stick and the slow, measured tread of the heavy, thickly-soled boots, of the big black and white collie dog closely to heel. "Sergeant," he called, and quickened his pace. "Sergeant!"

Questions, hopes, fears, welled in his heart, a torrent of words he tried desperately to arrange into some sort of sequence, but they never got past his lips. Taken by surprise, he bumped into Cluff when the Sergeant halted abruptly and a hand gripped his arm painfully in warning. Clive whimpered a greeting but he didn't hear it and the sounds in the street receded.

He looked where the Sergeant was looking. A stallholder, frozen in the act of placing a final orange on the top of a yellow pyramid, stared avidly. In the recessed entrance to a small stationer's shop a girl wept silently.

He started, recognizing Janet Rigsby, and the shame of this public exhibition of her grief affected him as acutely as if he was the one responsible for it. An embarrassment held him in thrall, so that he didn't know which way to turn or how to escape.

She wasn't alone. Another girl of her own age, concerned, embarrassed too, an acquaintance or fellow-worker perhaps, leaned over her, trying to shield her with her body from the gaze of passers-by, who, if they noticed, averted their heads and looked anywhere but at the shop. He couldn't remember ever having seen anything like this before. Its occurrence in Gunnarshaw, whose people were notorious for their reticence and the suppression of their emotions, made it all the more remarkable and pathetic.

All at once he realised that he was alone in the middle of the flags, the stall-holder revivified, Janet Rigsby crossing the road, supported by her friend, the spell lifted, the life of the town resumed. He looked about suddenly for Cluff and saw him standing in the mouth of a ginnel, with the dog squatting beside him, leaning on his stick, his face set.

CHAPTER IV

What was the Sergeant waiting for? What was Barker waiting for? Why had he slept so badly? Why had he rushed, half-dressed, without breakfast, so certain of the event, to the police station? What event? Involving what man, what woman? How, on this spring day, could anything disturb the quiet, even tenor of existence?

Barker leaned against one wall of the tunnel through the buildings lining the High Street and Cluff leaned against the other, Clive between them. This was the Sergeant's post. No one considered it strange that they should be there, their absence the strangeness not their presence, the High Street the hub of Gunnarshaw's being, along which, sooner or later, all its inhabitants paraded themselves for inspection. Could the Sergeant read their thoughts and divine their motivations, merely from watching them? What went on in the minds behind those open, honest faces? How did they live, how behave, in the privacy of their own four walls?

A girl weeping, and why? Were the possibilities running through Cluff's mind, as they were through his? A young girl, to whom the little snags of living, the cut and thrust of existence, might appear the end of the world, today but not tomorrow, when everything would be forgotten in a press of new hopes and new disappointments. He was young himself and remembered being younger. A quarrel perhaps with her mother, some prohibition of freedom, a desire refused, a course of action expressly forbidden, a dictatorial curtailment of liberty, a denial that she was herself, a separate being, entitled to spread her wings and fly to her own damnation? An argument with a boy friend, the destruction of love? How many reasons could there be, as fleeting as this sun climbing higher above the rim of the moors? A girl, a woman, and Barker's heart contracted. He glanced at the Sergeant and were they thinking alike? Pregnant perhaps, a baby on the way, the growing fears at last confirmed beyond possibility of doubt? In springtime, with her father a local celebrity, her friends those daughters of Gunnarshaw society raised, as she had been, in comfortable middle-class circumstances, the whole town knowing her? He shuddered for her and dare he suggest it to Cluff but if he did what was it to them, concerned with other laws, no guardians of morals? The possibility appalled him, and how could it be possible? Why was it impossible? He searched his memory and remembered Patterson at the cottage last night asking, "She's got a boy?" and Cluff refuting the question. Was the Sergeant always right? Did he know everything? Hadn't he been wrong – about people – before?

The tide of activity in the street ebbed and flowed, its cycles strongly marked, the workers vanishing to their desks and counters, an interval of calm, then the rising wave of morning shoppers, receding in its turn. In the shadows, hunger made him cold and mocked the sun shining on the windows of the bank across the road. "She works there," the Sergeant said, and Barker knew he was troubled too. He tried to reject these useless imaginings, to concentrate on the concrete, on his own discomfort and his foolishness, on those essentials that applied only to him.

Cluff's movement roused him from the coma into which he'd fallen. His blood pounded in his veins and he hadn't been mistaken, not last night nor in any of his fears since waking this morning. The ambulance driving up the street went on but Mole's car behind slowed and drew broadside on the setts, partly out of the stream of traffic. The Inspector leaned from his driving seat to the nearside front door and flung it open to speak to the Sergeant. The stall-holder's face, as Barker passed him, was a study in interest and curiosity and other people on the pavements had halted inquisitively.

The dog sat in the back of the car already and Barker joined him there. Cluff fitted his bulk with difficulty beside Mole and they set off in the same direction as the ambulance. For some reason the detective-constable believed they'd branch left after they'd passed the church, along the road that would bring them to the Secondary Modern School, but they continued straight on and at the next junction, of which one branch led to the Sergeant's cottage, they took the other.

The ambulance slowed deliberately to allow them to overtake and Mole, with sundry blasts of his horn and an appropriate display of signals, edged carefully in front of it. He didn't repeat whatever he'd said to Cluff before Barker had come to himself in the ginnel and they travelled in silence, the Sergeant's black mood impregnating the atmosphere in the little car with gloom.

The road dipped and soared, crossing the undulations of a narrow, uneven valley floor squashed between precipitous slopes that rose to high, craggy fells. Grey stone walls netted the lower pastures, which merged above with moorland, and the hills closed in, almost to a gorge.

"Stop!"

The Inspector trod on his brakes and behind them the tyres of the ambulance screeched. A steel snowplough, ready when need be for attachment to the front of a lorry, leaned, half-tipped on its side, against a pile of chippings in a road maintenance lay-by cut out of the grass verge. A small car, which Barker had seen before, parked behind it.

The Inspector looked angry: "They didn't tell me about this."

"No reason why anyone should – not yet: it's hardly midday," and the Sergeant got out and tried a door of the car, which opened at his touch. Over his shoulder Barker saw the ignition key in place, a ring dangling from it holding others. The fuel gauge indicated a tank half full of petrol. A rug lay on the rear seat and a toy tiger stretched on the ledge of the window above it.

Cluff stepped back and put his hand on the bonnet. Mole, taking his place at the car door, reached gingerly, protecting his fingers with a handkerchief, for the glove compartment and disclosed its contents. "Don't," the Sergeant said, and the Inspector's hand halted in mid-motion. "Leave it."

"We ought to lock it, at least," the Inspector protested, looking at the keys dangling from the dashboard.

"No one'll touch it," and Cluff waved Barker and Clive back into the minicar.

They drove a little farther, trailed faithfully by the ambulance, round a corner beyond which the road continued straight for a considerable distance, avenued by trees. A

rutted track, grass-grown between the depressions made by
wheels, diverged on the right at an angle of some forty-five
degrees. Farther along, where the space between it and the
road increased, a block of four cottages stood centrally in their
patches of garden.

An elderly man sitting on top of the wall near the mouth
of the track jumped down and waved at them, a deerstalker on
his head above a rough, weathered face sporting a ragged, grey
moustache. He wore a Norfolk-style jacket, its elbows patched
with cracked leather and its cuffs bound with it, and knee-
breeches fitting into canvas gaiters over the bottoms of which
brown leather boots were laced. He came to the window of
the car and said, "You can get across the field if you like, but
it's not so good."

"Wait for me," Cluff told Mole, and got out a second time.

"What the deuce?"

"Luke," the Sergeant addressed the man and exchanged
a few words with him before they walked off up the road to
the cottages. Barker, watching them through the windscreen,
noticed double wires extending from the line of telephone
poles bordering the verge to the nearest of the houses. "Who
would have thought," the Inspector asked, while they waited,
"when we were sitting with them at tea yesterday, that this
would happen?" and Barker wanted to reply, "Didn't you?" but
he restrained himself.

The minutes lengthened and the sky didn't look as bright
as it had been. "He must live there," the Inspector said for
the sake of making conversation. "I suppose that's where he
telephoned the station from."

"Who is he?"

"Luke Cracknell's his name, he said, and told us he works on the estate, looking after things in the plantations."

Barker's eyes had returned to the side-window and he wound it down in order to see better, sticking his head out: "They've made a shambles of it up there."

As far as they could see along the upper slopes back in the direction of Gunnarshaw the land was scarred, bare, denuded except for an odd tree-trunk here and there, looking from this distance like matchsticks. The steep declivity, plunging from crags on the skyline, reminded Barker in its nakedness and desolation of pictures he'd seen of shell-torn no-man's lands in the old war, or of a lunar landscape.

"The estate's got business men in charge now," Mole said, "not country gentry," and he laughed a little. "They didn't make much from those trees, if what I've heard's correct. It cost as much to get them down to the road as they could be sold for."

Was that then why the plantations began again, almost at right angles to where they sat? But the trees looked small too, as if perhaps they hadn't grown to maturity. Barker wondered how they could grow at all in the winds that blew on these fells, how they succeeded in remaining upright, rooted as they were in only the few inches of poor soil covering the hard rock.

Was plantation the right word, or wood? Forest, rather. The trees covered the other slopes towards the head of the dale and crowded down nearly to their feet, an endless mass of conifers, exactly alike, the geometrical plan of their arrangement still visible, though their branches had begun to intermingle and weave into a black carpet on the hills. A naked spur of ground jutted through the otherwise impenetrable blanket hiding the irregularities of the surface beneath, crowned by the ruins of an ancient watch-tower outlined against the sky behind.

The horn of the ambulance interrupted his meditations. It went on blowing, evidently to attract his attention and Mole's, and in the end they noticed Cluff and Cracknell walking from the back door of the cottage across its kitchen garden and climbing the palings that separated it from the track, up which they set off without a backward glance. Clive began to whimper beside Barker and he opened the door of the car and let the dog go and watched it race after the Sergeant.

"Just like him," the Inspector snorted, and experimented with the track but the ruts were too wide for his wheelbase and too deep, so that the bottom of the car scraped and rattled. He swore and ordered Barker out and refused the lift the driver of the ambulance offered them. They trudged in its wake, the ground increasingly muddy, cut to pieces in the past by large, heavily-loaded vehicles.

The track continued for some distance on its original line, past the cottages, through a pasture or two, where cows gazed at them with limpid eyes, and then curved sharply, driving for the bottom of the tree-covered fells, where a deep, narrow ghyll slashed them like a hatchet cut. Inclining steeply in its lower portion, it rose almost perpendicularly at its upper end, white water cascading over a lip of rock near the summit of the moor, plunging in a cloud of spray and foam, disappearing where the trees closed in. The track met the stream fed by the fall at a rough, trestle bridge, beginning to disintegrate, built by the woodcutters, leading to a dirt road through the wood on the Gunnarshaw side to where the tree-felling operations had taken place. Cluff and his companion and Clive waited for them there, together with the ambulance driver and his attendant, who held a folded stretcher.

They didn't cross the bridge, but made their way up the nearer bank of the stream, at first on level ground. After a short distance they had to clamber between the hill and the water but the passage opened up suddenly into a bowl-like, flat-bottomed depression, grassy and shaded with hazels and bushes with large green berries whose name Barker didn't know, a pleasant, secret dell, with springy turf, bordered by the singing stream. He stared with surprise at a wooden hut, fronted by a little railed verandah, like the pavilion of a small and inexpensive tennis club. Its door, slightly off centre, and its two glazed front windows looked tightly secured. Mole, who'd been bursting with the question, asked Cluff, "What did you phone about?"

"The car on the road."

The Sergeant and Cracknell pushed on easily for the farther side of the hollow, Clive ranging ahead, into the upper part of the ghyll. The stream ran threadlike here, very swiftly, no path along its bank, and they had to scramble through tangled bracken dividing water from trees before they emerged on to a higher shelf where the waterfall they'd seen from below, seventy or eighty feet of it, dived into a wide pool draining through a jumble of rocks at its outlet into the stream whose course they'd followed.

"I didn't touch it," Cracknell said. "I could see there wasn't any cause to."

The Sergeant called Clive to him and Mole and Barker and the ambulance men stood wide-eyed.

"It's deep," the forester added, about the pool. "The bottom's rock. Nearer the fall it mightn't have come up under the weight of water but anywhere in the middle it was bound to rise."

No one else moved so Barker stepped forward a tentative pace or two, only to be called back by the Sergeant.

"It was chance," Cracknell went on, unperturbed. "I mightn't have come by here for a month. People walk in the ghyll sometimes at weekends but not often to this spot." He looked up at the waterfall. "And there's no way down from above unless you jump."

The body curved round a rock, jammed hard against it by the force of the water funnelling from the pool, a wave building up and ripples curling away on either side. Its arms and legs shuddered without any cessation of motion, a little below the surface, and its hair drifted straight from the crown of its head like the neb of a cap.

CHAPTER V

The sun moved to its zenith but, even when directly overhead, did it ever penetrate here? The roar of the fall filled their ears and wet Barker's face with its spray, blown on an unwarmed wind. The serried ranks of trees stood sentinel, black and colourless, and however often he dragged his eyes from the pool they returned there of themselves. Her skirt had ridden to her hips: her blouse ballooned about her breasts: those movements of her limbs continued, pleadingly, as if she begged for help. They couldn't leave her where she was. What did they sit so quietly for, making no attempt to go to her rescue?

Someone was coming up the ghyll, not alone, an army by the sound of it. A girl's head appeared first, its features elfin, jet black hair long and wind-tossed, followed by a tiny, slim body clothed in sweater and trousers, moving like quicksilver, slithering, snakelike. Other-worldly, ethereal, some spirit of the hills, eyes bright and flashing, she led a column made up of the police surgeon and two constables Barker recognized as the crew of a police car, together with a gaunt civilian sweating profusely.

Her figure was like a boy's and if he touched her, Barker thought, she would vanish. He clutched harder at sanity, trying to tighten his grip on the mundane, but there was an agelessness in the place, a memory of times past that swamped those present. He sensed a long-forgotten relation between man and nature, an animistic belief, a closeness of the elemental, soul calling to soul. Death, if it existed, had no importance, this afterworld a haunt of ghosts and goblins, the very trees and stream with voices and personalities, the girl herself more sprite than mortal, mysterious as the pool, never to be caught however long pursued.

The Inspector sighed. "You were very sure," he said, in a tone quite unlike his own, empty of sarcasm.

"I sent for them when I phoned," the Sergeant replied.

"Because of the car?"

"Wasn't it obvious we'd need them?"

"I'm getting too old for this," Doctor Hamm complained. "Won't you speak to your murderers and persuade them to kill in more accessible spots?"

The girl drifted here and there, dipping her hands in the fall, touching the bushes and the trees, death too natural to be disturbing, watched by Cracknell's eyes with a far-away, remote, sad expression, a pride mingled with regret, an incomprehension. Time lost its meaning: everything went with an incredible slowness.

The photographer unpacked the boxes the constables had carried for him, setting up his tripod and focusing his camera, and the flash bulbs exploded in shattering bursts. Barker, at last, his feet slipping on the rocks, his shoes filling with icy water, his fingers bent into hooks, dragged her ashore. They laid her on the bank and Hamm examined her. "When?" Cluff asked.

"Last night."

"She had a husband," Barker said.

"She worked," Mole interrupted, a meaning in his voice as there had been in the detective-constable's.

"She's dead," Hamm stated flatly.

"Drowned?"

"Did you send for me to ask me that?" He pointed to her neck, faintly bruised. "Once I have her on the slab it'll be the easiest thing in the world to prove she wasn't."

"Didn't anyone care enough to report her missing?" Barker demanded.

"Too many people," the Sergeant answered, and nodded at the ambulance men.

They loaded her on a stretcher and the girl had somehow vanished into the trees. Coming out of the ghyll by the hut was like coming out of a pit and when they reached the road they found Hamm's car and the police car drawn up there too.

"But how will you get back?" the Inspector asked, reluctant, when the ambulance and the other vehicles had driven away, to leave the Sergeant behind.

"By now," Cluff said, "they'll have towed her car in."

"She wasn't alone, that's certain."

"Why was it left there, half a mile down the road from where the track begins?"

"It might tell us something."

"Perhaps."

The Inspector's eyes narrowed: "Then we'll meet in Gunnarshaw?"

"Sometime."

"It's less trouble to keep him occupied. He likes to help," Cluff said, as Mole buzzed away in his minicar, and he turned

to Cracknell, who was still with them. The forester led them
without speaking, the Sergeant beside him, Barker and Clive
behind, to the gate of his cottage and the chimneys of the
three beyond it were smokeless, their gardens unkempt. He
took them into a living-room not unlike Cluff's though less
colourful, where a fire burnt brightly in the grate. Cups and
plates of pastries stood ready on its table, with the girl who'd
met them at the pool waiting to serve them. Barker put his
shoes to dry in the hearth and remembered that he'd had no
breakfast.

"Those cottages are still empty," Cluff said.

"They always will be," Cracknell replied.

"You're here."

"So long as one man has to do the work of four."

"They'll never get you out."

"Only feet first."

"You'd buy this place if you had to?"

"The people next door weren't sorry to go. Their wives
didn't like it. If the new owners ever decided to give my men
their jobs back they'd get no takers."

"We have to depend on you then."

"I heard nothing last night."

"You're always about, in the plantings, up the ghyll."

"I mind my own business."

"You couldn't leave here if you wanted to. Abbie'd not be
happy anywhere else."

"I promised her mother," and Clive had gone to her, dog
and girl in communion.

"You're not frightened of me, Abbie," Cluff said, "no more
than Clive is," and she smiled, looking from him to Barker.

"He won't hurt you either."

She asked, "Will they take the hut away now?"

"You don't like it?"

Her face grew sombre and her father said, "There's been trouble. Rigsby complained she watched him."

"Did it matter?"

"Not to his wife and daughter."

"But to you," the Sergeant told Abbie. "You're right," he agreed. "Why did he want to put it there? Couldn't he have gone further from Gunnarshaw if he had to have a weekend retreat?"

"Not in surroundings like those," Barker said.

"It doesn't improve them. Abbie knows." Cluff stared at the girl. "Was it the hut or the people?"

"The people."

"Any people?"

"Only him and people like him."

"Not Janet?"

"Sometimes I talked with her."

"She enjoyed coming?"

"It frightened her."

"And Mrs Rigsby?"

"He didn't bring her with him much."

"They aren't all like him, Abbie. Who else?"

"I'm glad she's dead."

"Who killed her?"

The girl gazed at him for a moment and then ran out of the room. "Clive!" Cluff ordered sharply, and the dog stopped unwillingly, giving Abbie time to close the door behind her before he could follow. "Animals can't keep away from her,"

Cracknell said.

"She's seen something."

"Who knows what she knows?" Her father frowned. "She's always in the hills. If she doesn't want to talk you'll get nothing out of her."

"How long has it been in the ghyll?"

"Since last summer."

"He comes often?"

"You'd wonder why he spent the money on it."

"At nights?"

"Cars pass on the road. They stop where the track branches off, out of the way of anything else going by. It needn't be him every time."

"You haven't seen that woman before?"

"Only in the street at Gunnarshaw."

"Let me know if Abbie says anything," and the Sergeant got up while Barker put his shoes on. "We'll go out at the back."

Cracknell saw them through the empty scullery and over the fence and when they reached the hut again Barker imagined movement amongst the bushes on the rim of the bowl in which it stood: "Is she mad?"

"No more than we are. Three hundred years ago she'd have been burnt for a witch but not by the people hereabouts."

"Her mother?"

"There's only her father and her." The Sergeant examined the turf. "It wouldn't show, however many people had been here. In any case they'd have to walk from the bridge, from the road if they'd only a small car."

A hasp and staple, with a padlock, secured the door. The

Sergeant tested the lock and the screws in the woodwork and the windows were of casement type, with a catch on one leaf fitting into a socket on the other. He felt in his pocket and produced a clasp-knife whose blade he inserted into the crack where the leaves of one of the windows joined. He pressed it upwards against the catch, which lifted easily, pulling at the frame, opening the window outwards. He said, "A child could get in," but a man of size couldn't, though Barker managed to.

The hut had two rooms, in the first a table and some folding canvas chairs, a low cupboard with crockery and pans and lamps on its shelves, a double-burner primus stove with a can of kerosene beside it. The Sergeant moved along the verandah outside as Barker went into the second room, which contained a large iron bedstead provided with a mattress covered with a scuffed, creased blanket but no other bedclothes. The mat on the floor was concertinaed and a long bag, which proved to contain a dismantled camp-bed, lay in one corner as though it had fallen from the wall which propped it up. Through its closed front window Cluff saw Barker's mouth working as he stood by the window in the rear wall immediately opposite the one by which the Sergeant waited. When he got round to the back the second window was open and Barker said, "It wasn't fastened."

"But shut."

"It could have been pushed to from outside."

"Or Rigsby could have forgotten about the catch."

Barker looked at the bed and the mat: "Would he have left things like this?"

"You're not suggesting he climbed through his own window instead of coming in by the door?" The Sergeant leaned an elbow on the windowsill, his head in the room. "What are you suggesting?"

"Mrs Fairchild worked with him," and Barker's voice sounded uncertain. "She'd hardly be coming anywhere else. Not to Cracknell's and the other houses are empty."

"He's a rational man. This hut belongs to him. If he'd wanted to get rid of her wouldn't he have chosen somewhere not connected with him?"

"You're assuming he'd a reason," Barker said.

"Aren't you?"

"Yesterday—" and the detective-constable left the rest of his sentence unspoken.

"It's a start, at any rate."

CHAPTER VI

A single-decked red bus overtook them on the road and drew to a stop. The driver, who doubled as conductor, pulled the bar to open its door without leaving his seat behind the wheel: "A lift, Caleb?"

"I've got legs."

"Barker doesn't look so nimble. You're off your beat."

"It's all my beat, for twenty miles around."

"Something on foot, eh?"

"Me."

"If you want to keep it a secret – I'll hear about it in Gunnarshaw," and the driver crashed his door to.

Mrs Fairchild's car had gone from the lay-by. In a field over the wall young rabbits hopped in and out of a clump of trees. They passed the mouth of the lane they'd driven down to the tip where parts of Miss Axminster had been dug up last year[*] and beyond the inn nearby the first houses of Gunnarshaw came into view, on a hill to their right, where they could see, too, the other road that led to and from Cluff's cottage. Near the centre of the town they had the choice of turning towards the Modern School or of going straight on to the High Street but Mole's car came round the corner by the church and the Inspector saw them. He stopped and they crossed to him.

[*]   *More Deaths for Sergeant Cluff*

"I wouldn't trust Rigsby," Mole said, "but we've found no prints on the car that aren't probably hers. The handbag I saw in the glove compartment belongs to her."

"Where are you going – home?"

The Inspector reddened: "I didn't know what time you'd get back. I'm on my way to the school."

"You knew the hut was Rigsby's?"

"I'd heard he had one somewhere close to the town."

"It didn't take us much more than half an hour to walk back," the Sergeant said.

"No one had asked about her up to my leaving the station just now."

"Is it the headmaster's job to look for her?"

"You'd have thought he'd have been interested. You're coming along?"

"I'll leave it to you."

The Sergeant and Barker, with Clive, carried on into the High Street, which basked in the afternoon sun, more crowded now than in the morning, the owner of the fruit-stall by the ginnel plying a good trade. The atmosphere lacked any current of excitement and evidently the news hadn't got out so far, that treat still in store for the gossips. "If Hamm was right—" the detective-constable mused aloud, and Cluff interrupted, "He's always right."

"Then she must have been out all night," Barker replied. "If she'd been your wife wouldn't you have been worried?"

"I'm not Fairchild."

"He'll have been home to his dinner too."

"They've no family. Probably she has hers at school and he eats in the town."

"He ought to be told."

"You think so?"

Barker considered and decided, "No. The longer he waits the stranger it is." A thought struck him. "Unless he's taken to his heels."

"He didn't have to go all that way to kill her."

"He did to hide her body."

"And left her car in plain view on the roadside?"

"Can he drive?" but the Sergeant had halted outside the entrance to one of the banks. He leaned on his stick like a man who didn't intend to move in the near future and said, instead of answering Barker's question, "You know where he works."

Barker waited a while and then started to walk off, asking over his shoulder, "If he does try to leave the town?"

"Will you let him?"

Cluff looked up at the church clock and it was almost three: Clive nudged his fingers on the handle of his walking-stick: Barker receded along the pavement, hurrying. The Sergeant wondered if he ever knew when he began how much he would dig up extraneous to the prime object, things that once brought to light couldn't be hidden. Once the wheels rolled he couldn't stop them, whoever got in their way.

He stood until the first notes of the hour chimed before he turned and pushed past the messenger who was in the act of closing the bank door. The counter, as he'd hoped, was clear of customers and he could choose his clerk from the five ranged along it. Clive's claws scraped on the tiled floor.

The movable sign, still brightly new, read "Miss J. Rigsby," and he said he'd forgotten his cheque book but she merely stared at him with dry, red-rimmed eyes deep-set in her pale face and, despite her sturdy, muscular figure, she looked ill. When she gave him the single cheque he asked for her hand trembled and she dropped one of the coins with which he paid for it. The clerk in the position next to hers, whose sign was lettered "Mr W. Stockwell," went down on his knees to find it for her, taking as much trouble as if she'd lost a golden sovereign instead of a copper penny. The Sergeant made out his cheque to himself, for five pounds he didn't want in his pocket, writing slowly and watching them from under lowered eyelids.

Her hands still shook as she counted out his notes. He couldn't miss Will Stockwell's concern but if they were thrown into each other's company by their work he'd never seen them together outside the bank. He counted the years since the Rigsbys moved to Gunnarshaw, three, four maybe, and when they came she'd hardly be out of puberty but the only man he'd ever noticed her with had been her father, walking in the fields round his cottage on Sunday afternoons, in the town on weekdays. It happened less and less frequently as time went on, Rigsby perhaps becoming more involved with local concerns, but her mother had never accompanied them at all. Had he congratulated the pair in those early days on their closeness and warmed to the relationship between parent and child, or had he been troubled even then by the girl's adoration of her father, the manner in which she clung to him, the expression in her eyes when she looked at him?

He realized that he, not the girl, was the object now of scrutiny by the bank staff and his head came up slowly, his eyes resting on her. She shrank back against the screen separating the space behind the counter from a general office occupying the remainder of the floor, her hand going to her mouth, and he knew fear when he saw it. Stockwell's gaze at him was hostile, mutely threatening.

He stuffed the pound notes into a pocket. Why was she afraid of him today when she hadn't been afraid of him yesterday at the school? It had been something else then, nothing that pleased him but not, either, like this. And yet, whatever it was, had it pointed inevitably, if only he'd been able to recognize it, to today's discovery?

CHAPTER VII

With Clive beside him he rounded the corner at the bottom of the High Street, pursued by the shrewd glances and the whispers of the passers-by, a disturbance beginning to build up in the atmosphere of the town though as yet the billboards outside the newsagents' shops carried no news of murder. A brass plate set in the entrance to a flight of stairs indicated the nature of the offices above and beyond it cookers and electrical gadgets filled a large display window. Barker stepped into his path and said, "He's there."

The Sergeant passed him to the stairs and climbed slowly to a landing with glass-panelled doors. He peered between black letters reading "Accounts" at a counter inside one of the rooms and past it to where half a dozen people or more, both men and women, lounged at desks. With one exception they seemed not to have a care in the world, smoking, chatting, laughing together, sipping from cups of tea, handing to each other a tin of biscuits, ledgers open in front of them but ignored, even the pretence of work wearing thin. Only the man at the desk in the farthest corner divorced himself from this happy state of affairs, no more occupied than the rest of them but preferring to spend his leisure in a different misogynic way. He sat with his elbows on the desk and his chin cupped in the palms of his hands, staring at nothing, an anachronism, something out of the pages of Dickens, a character from a counting house in the bad old days. The oldest of them all, an air about him advertised that in status he was the most junior, lacking the brashness of the men that passed for ability and the femininity of the girls that, when it came to the push, perhaps rendered ability unnecessary. He was grey and balding, unimpressive in stature, a silky moustache far from emphasizing his maleness only underlining his failure as a man, and his clothes were as worn as himself. The troubles of the universe weighed on his shoulders and dug furrows in his face and his colleagues had given him up long ago and so, too, had probably everyone who knew him, including those who should have been nearest and dearest.

Cluff retraced his steps to the bottom of the stairs, where Clive was waiting. He left Barker there and wandered along the pavement without responding to the greetings of his acquaintances, his feet dragging a little, steering automatically for the police station, where the Duty Constable watched him wordlessly into the C.I.D. room.

"Come in," the Sergeant said, and the Duty Constable walked across the floor and put a mug of tea on the Sergeant's table: "I'll send out for some sandwiches if you like."

Cluff hadn't taken his hat off or removed his Burberry: his stick lay on the table and his dog lay under it. He didn't answer and, "A mess?" the constable asked.

"It will be before we've done."

"Killing's always nasty—"

"Nastier for some reasons than others."

"—especially when it's people you know."

"They're people in any case."

"You can't help it."

The Sergeant reached for the telephone and dialled a number: "Hamm?"

"You're back then?" the receiver said. "Someday you'll have us both in court – and not in the witness box. When do I get a post-mortem order? Nobody's made a formal identification."

"It'll come."

"I hope so. Anyhow, I've put her back together again. Sex, female: age, thirty-five to forty: in non-technical terms, never a mother and no signs of being one – in fact, there's a bar to pregnancy, slight and operable, but evidently it hadn't troubled her. Cause of death, strangulation, the pressure applied from behind. Lungs free of water. No marks of a struggle – presumably she was taken by surprise. Does that put you in the picture, or did you have it clear already?"

"What sort of strangulation?"

"Ah!"

"Well?"

"We're not as international as that yet – thank God! – in spite of black faces and brown on the streets. Not thuggee but something pretty like it – a good job, either by accident or design."

"Easier than manual?"

"Simpler. A rope – in this case, probably a length of thin material – a deft twist and the worst's over. It's only a matter of turning the screw after that."

"But a child couldn't do it."

"A child couldn't reach. It could have been done when she was lying down, I suppose, but I'm assuming she was standing up. That satisfies you?"

"I'm in no position to argue."

"And I've my practice to attend to. I'd be grateful this time if you'd confine things to a single killing: your murders have a habit of becoming cumulative."

The Sergeant replaced the receiver and looked steadily at the Duty Constable, who asked, "Does it fit?"

"It's too early to say."

"She wasn't much of a character."

Cluff leaned back in his chair and dug his hands into the pockets of his coat: "They don't allow me a scale of guilt. It's all or nothing."

"Fairchild did his best."

"I've been sorry for him too. It astonished me they went on living in that house."

"Hobnobbing with hoi polloi?" and the Duty Constable grinned mirthlessly.

The Sergeant went on staring at him for a long time before asking, "Will your wife be in?"

The constable nodded: "She's the one to go to," but there was no malice in his tone. "Mrs Knowall: I'm not in the same class with her." He stood aside to let the Sergeant pass and gave Clive a pat as the dog went by. In the outer office he waited until the street door closed and then went to the window, watching their progress down the street for as long as he could see them.

"But why there in the ghyll?" the Sergeant asked himself as he walked, and the question he'd put to Barker already, earlier in the afternoon, nagged at him. He couldn't forget the car either and he searched his memory to remember its make,

turning on impulse into a garage that was agent for its sale.
He passed the petrol pumps in the forecourt and a window
whose glass shielded a couple of new models and entered the
workshop proper with its lubrication lift and its inspection
pit, its benches and tools. Legs cased in blue overalls stiff with
grease protruded from underneath a small van but he ignored
them and, after glancing into an empty cubicle used as an
office, continued on into the shadows, where a lamp at the
end of a cable, its bulb protected by wire mesh, hung on a
hook, directing its light at a bench.

The proprietor put his file down and twirled the handle
of a vice with one hand, removing with the other a piece
of metal on which he'd been working. He glanced round at
Cluff and nodded at the dog and held the metal, its surface
bright, at eye-level, squinting along it. He laid it down on the
workbench and reached for an oil-soaked rag, with which he
rubbed his dirt-encrusted fingers. "You haven't come to it at
last?" he said, cramming the rag into his hip pocket. "Is that
Morris of yours still running?"

"It would if I wanted it to," Cluff replied.

"Give it to a museum. I've got a little job you can have
cheap."

"And pay a fortune in repairs for ever afterwards?"

The garageman simulated disappointment: "I'm in trouble
then?"

"You're the best of a bad lot," the Sergeant said. "You must
be if folk like Fairchild deal with you."

"You're barking up the wrong tree there, Caleb. When it
comes to motors he's as daft as you are."

"He bought one off you."

"His wife did."

"It's the same thing."

"Not these days it isn't."

"He'd pay for it, anyhow."

"On what he gets? With what she costs him in other ways?"

"It's in her name then?"

"The agreement is. It's still part mine for the next six months."

"Handy, at any rate, when she's got someone to share the driving."

"You don't think Fairchild's any good at that? I'd rather trust myself with you. He can't drive."

"How much would you allow me," Cluff said, "if I traded in the Morris?"

"Come off it, Caleb. A self-respecting scrap-yard wouldn't take it as a gift."

"You've lost a customer apart from me," the Sergeant told him, "but in your trade and at what you charge I daresay you'll survive."

The shadows lengthened and he stood on the kerb, with no plan and no set course of action, groping in the fog shrouding his mind, not really wanting it to lift. When the Inspector's minicar appeared in the distance he dived into a stationer's shop, from which he didn't emerge until Mole had gone past.

He glanced at the Stop Press and flung the paper into a waste-basket attached to the shaft of a lamp standard. The town still didn't know, but, if it did, it would look at him and imagine him busy, his wanderings purposeful, the thoughts in his head clear. Soon, when the news broke, they'd give him a wide berth in the streets, concerned not to disturb his preoccupation, digging each other in the ribs, peeping at him out of the corners of their eyes, nodding wisely. He felt like a charlatan with his dog and his stick and his old clothes that got older as the years went by. Who was he trying to deceive, himself or them?

Motion, at least, put up a show of capability and when he came to himself again he was at the gates of the school.

The children had gone and no one moved on the playing fields, a silence as of mourning enveloping the buildings, the parking lot empty of vehicles. He pushed through a door into a cloakroom forested with coat-pegs and from there into a long corridor. From somewhere in the place the handle of a bucket rattled and the rays of the evening sun made bars through the vastness of glass comprising the outer walls, stabbing at the doors of classrooms ranged down the vista in front of him. The list of a netball team signed with Mrs Fairchild's name stood out from a collection of notices pinned to a board on his right.

Lodge bumped into him as he turned into a recess from which the stairs mounted. They parted and backed from each other and stared, both their faces serious. The deputy headmaster said, "Inspector Mole was here."

"I'm sorry."

"People will forget."

"You've taught here for a long time," Cluff said.

"Since the school opened."

"Things aren't as they were when I was a boy."

"The system changes."

"It's been a success?"

"In this school. Rigsby's predecessor put it on its feet."

"You helped too."

"I did what I could."

"But they brought in an outsider—"

"When has a prophet honour in his own country?" Lodge shrugged. "Rigsby's a good man." A shadow crossed his face. "It might have been different if my wife had lived."

The Sergeant said, "Was that why you weren't appointed?"

"Have you ever heard of a bachelor headmaster, especially in a mixed school?"

"You won't marry again?"

"It's years ago."

The Sergeant's eyes moved to the flight of stairs.

"He hasn't gone home," Lodge added. "We've been talking about it together."

"She was popular?"

"It's hard to get teachers in a school like this."

"She must have been out of touch."

"We couldn't do without them, those wives who come back to the profession. If their methods are dated, their knowledge rusty, they've experience of the world."

"She's only lived in Gunnarshaw."

"*Faute de mieux*," Lodge said. "It falls on Rigsby's shoulders not mine."

"No trouble?"

"He's wise enough to make allowances." The deputy headmaster started to move off. "The town's got a high opinion of you. You'll sort it out."

The Sergeant climbed into the corridor on the upper floor and left Clive outside the door at which he knocked. "You—!" Rigsby exclaimed, his fingers tightening on the pen with which he was writing, and he repeated what Lodge had said, "The Inspector's been already."

Cluff sat down in a chair opposite to him: "She'd gone absent before without letting you know?"

"I was on the point of contacting her husband."

"How long since she started teaching again?"

"Winter last year. In January, after the Christmas holidays."

Foils and a fencing mask decorated the wall above the fireplace, in the hearth of which stood an electric fire, bowl-shaped, with a strong wire guard. "Yours?" the Sergeant asked.

"Relics of my youth. I used to be thought good at fencing – one of my better sports."

A portable typewriter in its case occupied a small table at right angles to one end of the desk and the study was comfortable, its furniture light, polished wood, its picture windows, with heavy curtains suspended in folds beside them, overlooking the playing fields. The pallor of the headmaster's face equalled that of his daughter in the bank and he'd changed, his bumptiousness gone. His voice sounded different: he didn't seem so big, as if he'd shrunk overnight, his whole manner deflated. "Is there nothing you can tell me?" Cluff said.

"She worked well. I'd no complaints—"

"You know where she was found?" and the Sergeant spoke softly, watching the face of the other man, the lips pressed tightly together. Footsteps in the corridor got louder and stopped, the person making them perhaps bending to Clive, then started again and receded. Cluff could hear the ticking of his watch, mingled with that of Rigsby's. "Had she been there?" he asked, and the headmaster's hands began to shake.

"The hut belongs to you."

The tip of a tongue licked dry lips: "For my wife and daughter." Rigsby swallowed. "Our garden at home's not private—"

"A pleasant spot," Cluff said, "in that part of the ghyll anyway. And easily accessible from Gunnarshaw. She takes her friends there?"

"Janet?"

"Not too far off to reach on foot. No neighbours – unless you count Cracknell and Abbie."

"You've seen them?"

"They've nothing in the way of information."

Rigsby released the breath he'd been holding; "The winter's hardly over – we haven't used it recently."

"Not up to the present," Cluff said, continuing from where his previous remark had left off.

"What?"

"Abbie's secretive," and the Sergeant took a few steps in the direction of the corridor. "She almost lives out of doors, winter and summer alike. She's not afraid of the dark."

"In a dream world, without time, without a sequence of events," Rigsby said. "Can she distinguish between facts and the fictions she invents? You couldn't rely on the word of a girl like that."

"You trespassed," Cluff murmured, "into her sanctuary," and the door closed behind him. He looked down at Clive, whose eyes fixed on a small, wizened man leaning, at the far end of the corridor from the headmaster's stairs, on a mop, by a right-angled bend into which he could scurry out of sight. He disappeared as the Sergeant approached and when Cluff

reached the corner he was standing at the top of a flight of
service stairs, carrying a bucket now in addition to the mop.
They went to the ground floor together and descended farther,
into the foundations of the building, to a windowless room,
all concrete, floor and walls and ceiling, whose close, foetid
atmosphere smelt, sickly, of warm fuel oil. Fatly lagged pipes
banked above their heads and the windows in the furnace
doors glowed white shot with red. The Sergeant said, "Rigsby
can't eat you."

"He can give me the sack."

"From what I know of you it's a marvel you ever got the
job."

"You're not fair, Mr Cluff."

"It's only because your father shepherded for mine, Elijah,
I've never put you away."

The small piggy eyes narrowed: "All that's behind me. I
needed a chance—"

"How did you know she was dead? It's not general
knowledge yet."

"The Inspector—"

"You listened at the door, and again just now."

"I'd the corridor to swab. Mr Lodge was in with them too."

"If they find out you'll have both of them to cope with."

"Not Mr Lodge – he's like me: he knows what it is to be
treated badly. Why did they bring Rigsby in as new headmaster
when he was on the spot?"

"Is that where your sympathy lies?"

"Rigsby knew her," the caretaker said.

"He had to."

"Better than that," and the disgust in the Sergeant's face

made Elijah rush on before he was stopped. "They've been alone in his study—"

"He wouldn't have made that mistake if he'd known you properly."

"Late into the night."

"Nobody from the town would, not with you working on the premises."

"It's true."

"Coming from you?"

"Ask his wife then. Ask Mr Lodge."

"Why don't you use it to wash your mouth out with?" the Sergeant asked, looking at the soapy water in the bucket.

CHAPTER VIII

He felt soiled, contaminated, both inside and out: a hatred of the school welled in him that had begun not today but twenty-four hours ago. Did the inanimate take on the character of those working with it, a building repel or attract according to the personalities of its occupants?

He sucked the evening air into his lungs and the dark closed in, a week yet before the clocks went forward to summertime. Where to? The idea of being alone in his cottage with his thoughts appalled him: rest and sleep alike had fled beyond possibility of capture. What did he care if anyone accused him of roaming the streets like a lost soul, glowering, unapproachable, morose? The business, like the penalty of its solution, concerned no one but himself.

Where to then, he asked himself a second time. Was there a difference, providing it was away from here? All the same, instead of returning to the main entrance of the school he crossed the playing fields and the pastures, climbing walls and fences until the river, its bed rubbish choked, presented a more formidable barrier. He walked along its bank and came to a bridge, scrambling up to the road it carried, on one side a council housing estate, on the other a cemetery in which more than one victim from the past was buried, where they would soon be digging a newer grave.

The lamps had come on in the main road south out of
Gunnarshaw when he reached it and he turned, not for the
centre of the town but away from it. Once under a railway
bridge, the houses stopped and over the low wall bordering
the pavement the canal looked stagnant and still. Across the
carriageway a train roared, invisible in the deep cutting of a
second line bridged, like the road, by the first. The houses
resumed where the canal here and the railway track there both
swung away at an angle, double rows of them with the traffic
flowing between. Beyond a mill, round a sharp bend, canal
and road drew together again, a steep, high bank covered with
stunted bushes running up to the towpath, facing a single
row of houses, the last in Gunnarshaw, continuing the line
of those he'd passed earlier. He swung into the gap between
it and the end of the adjoining row, on to a cindered path
between backyards and a wire fence bordering a field. A
solitary gas-lamp burnt halfway down the length of the row, a
man inclined against its fluted shaft in yellow, flickering light
too dim to make his features recognizable.

The Sergeant and Clive passed the small wooden gates
and the brief stretches of low wall alternating with the higher
walls of outhouses pierced by square openings closed with
iron plates through which the dustmen emptied the ash-pits.
A little wearily, Barker straightened and pointed across one
of the yards to an uncurtained window. Fairchild moved in
and out of view in the lighted room behind it and, "He came
straight here from his office," the detective-constable said.
"He didn't speak to anyone on the way. A couple of buses
passed him but he walked."

"Would he have stayed in the town if he'd killed her?"

Cluff asked.

"Can you tell from looking at him what he'd do? Has he any interest left in anything? What rules can you apply to a man who looks like that?"

Behind them a small, wooden shed, whose double doors faced the cinder path, obviously served as a garage. "Hasn't he even looked to see whether the car's there?" the Sergeant said.

"He let himself in with a key at the front," Barker replied. "He came into the yard once for a shovelful of coal from the coal-place. You can see from the smoke," and he looked up at the chimney, "that he's lit a fire."

"It's getting cold." Cluff made for the gate next to Fairchild's farther down the row. "You've been there long enough."

"If he goes out?"

"He won't."

The Duty Constable from the police station, in his shirt-sleeves, a broad leather belt holding up his dark-blue serge trousers, opened the back door to them: "By gum, Caleb, it's taken you a fair while to get here." He shouted, in stentorian tones, "How far will it stretch, lass? There's two of 'em and a dog."

From the scullery they entered a living-room to be greeted by a round dumpling of a woman with twinkling eyes. "All I want," Cluff said, "is a word or two," and she glanced at Barker: "Suit yourself, Caleb Cluff, but he's on his last legs. There's no call to work him to death." She ordered her husband, "Get their coats off," and disappeared into the pantry under the stairs.

The smell of frying sausages made Barker's mouth water and the sizzling of chips in deep fat was music to his ears. For a while, at any rate, Fairchild receded in importance, though he listened with one ear for sounds from next door while the other picked up the Duty Constable's monologue of pleasantries and his occasional interchanges with the woman in the scullery, whom he addressed as Dolly. The Sergeant sat with his boots on the fender, staring into the fire, and Clive had his muzzle noisily in a dish with which he'd already been served.

They held in this house to a strict order of priorities, no business begun until the inner man was attended to and Dolly had done the washing-up. The constable lay back in the armchair, blue smoke from strong-smelling twist wreathing about his head, a button eased on his waistband, facing Cluff across the hearthrug on which the dog stretched. Barker sat on a sofa, pulled from the wall nearer the fire for his benefit, warm and stuffed, well-fed, not only with the sausages but with a plethora of pastries and cheese and fruit cake offered with apologies for the absence of a pudding, and very drowsy. Dolly, on an armless, upright chair, between the sofa and Cluff, knitted busily, the click of her needles increasing the detective-constable's somnolence.

"This wasn't a social visit," the Sergeant protested.

"Let it sort itself out," the Duty Constable answered.

"It's what Harry always does," his wife interrupted, throwing a quizzical look at her husband.

"Life's short," the constable said. "It wants taking easy."

"If he's not in that chair," Dolly added, "he's down in his allotment. What he knows about the Fairchilds wouldn't fill a thimble."

"One gossip in the family's enough," and Harry drew comfortably on his pipe.

"They were as different as chalk and cheese," the Sergeant said. "It's a mystery to me how she picked a husband like that."

"He wore trousers. Seventeen or eighteen years ago, anyway, he wasn't much different from anyone else." Dolly's needles moved so fast that Barker could scarcely follow them. "He'd just come out of the army. She only taught in an elementary school and her parents weren't any better than his."

"But it lasted," Cluff argued.

"It always does in Gunnarshaw – on the surface – with people like us."

"She'd have left me long ago but she couldn't face the scandal," Harry put in.

His wife continued, "That woman wore him down. She needed babies."

"We'd five," the Duty Constable told Barker. "They're all married now and this place is filled with grandchildren week in and week out. The station's the only spot where I get any peace."

"It's him they come to see," Dolly said. "He's soft." Her face grew serious. "I could have cried sometimes at what she was doing to Fairchild. She couldn't see it but that didn't make it any better. She destroyed him, like water wearing away a stone. He'd nothing left, no push, no ambition, no self-respect. She nagged him until she convinced him he wasn't good enough for her."

"He should have clouted her," the constable said.

"He loved her. He went on loving her. He'd made his own bed and he's the sort who'd lie on it." Dolly's needles stopped. "She didn't understand that if he got nowhere it was because of what she was doing to him. He gave her every penny he earned. He spent nothing on himself. She'd only to ask and he got what she wanted some way."

"As long as he could," Harry amended.

"She was never satisfied. In the end she finished the job off by going back to work and he couldn't even pretend he was the man in that house. She bought the car and she never finished telling him that what he ought to have provided she was paying for herself."

"Even a worm can turn," Barker thought.

"He went on trying," Dolly continued. "For years she'd been complaining about having to go on living in a row like this. They were going to move. He'd got her a semi-detached out your way, Caleb."

"They're not cheap."

"He'd worked miracles for her before. And she still wiped her feet on him."

"More than that," the Sergeant said, and stared at the constable's wife.

She didn't say anything for a while, and then: "It had to come."

"You knew?"

"She worked with men."

"So it didn't do him any good, after all," Barker commented, unable to keep quiet. "Not even the new house."

Harry frowned. He leaned forward to tap the bowl of his pipe against the bars of the grate and his tone was flat: "Fairchild would put up with anything and come back for more." He glared at them. "Who says she was playing about? I've heard nothing about it and isn't the husband always the last to know?"

CHAPTER IX

Dolly wouldn't accept their thanks for the meal. Harry accompanied them into the yard and they stood, the three men and the dog, in the patch of light from the living-room window, the sky velvety, studded with stars, a nip in the air no longer unpleasant now that their stomachs were full. "Was that what you wanted to hear?" the Duty Constable asked, and added, "You wouldn't have got it from me."

"I didn't want to hear anything," the Sergeant replied. "But I'd no alternative."

They closed the back gate behind them and Harry leaned on it, watching them, shrugging wordlessly when Cluff turned to look at him.

How long, Barker wondered, did the Sergeant intend to stand there, and he felt himself torn by the old conflict, the need to protect Cluff in his official capacity, to ensure that the policeman acted like the policeman and was seen to do so, and the realization of the price owed to duty. He walked himself to Fairchild's gate and opened it noisily. Harry didn't move and he thought that the Sergeant wasn't going to either but when they were at Fairchild's door he tried to convince himself that there'd never been any doubt of their ultimate objective.

Did he expect an answer to their knock? The blind on the

window had been drawn since they last looked but a thin strip of light outlined its edges. It meant nothing, the house empty or, worse, the occupant beyond their help. He had to take a firm grip on himself before he could believe in the reality of the man confronting them, who stood aside without speaking and motioned them in.

A few coals smouldered smokily in the fireplace: a teapot, a cup and saucer, a loaf of bread, a jar of jam, on the table could have been taken in themselves as evidence of a poverty that couldn't afford even a sufficiency of food, but it wasn't like that at all. The house, in the vernacular used by Gunnarshaw, was a palace, every stick of its furniture expensive, each appointment reeking of money. They trod on a thick-piled, fitted carpet and the cost of the suite must have run into three figures. A wide-screened, console television set in one corner faced a combined radio and record player in another. A heavy embossed paper hung on the walls. The surround of the fire could have been compared to advantage with any to be found in the town. Amongst all this luxury Fairchild drooped, strayed into an alien world, a weed amongst flowers, a fish out of water, a pig amongst pearls.

"She hasn't come back," the Sergeant said. "Her car isn't in the garage. You haven't seen her since yesterday and it'll soon be tomorrow." He waited without result for a reply. "Didn't it occur to you to try to find her?" and Fairchild still said nothing. "Did she live her own life to that extent?" His eyes wandered round the room: "How did you manage it?" and came finally to rest on the man's threadbare clothing, his cracked shoes with their wafer-thin soles, his too-long hair, the dandruff on his shiny shoulders. "She's dead. After all this, she's dead. After

what you've given her, after what you've done to satisfy her,
though she'd never be satisfied, even after that final sacrifice
of the house you were going to put her into."

Barker leapt to catch him as he tottered and Fairchild lay
limp in his arms for a moment before he pushed weakly, trying
to escape. The detective let go and Cluff said, "You're free.
Can't you realize that? – you're free."

"It's too late," and they could scarcely hear him.

"It's never too late."

"There's nothing without her," Fairchild said. "I never
interfered. We'd no children either."

The Sergeant remembered what Hamm had told him on
the telephone: "Did she make you believe that was your fault
too?"

Fairchild stumbled to a chair, into which he collapsed. He
buried his face in his hands, his shoulders heaving, and said,
"You'll have to arrest me. You've no choice." His sobs mounted
in volume until the whole room, the entire house, seemed to
vibrate with them. They went on and on, unbearably, until
Barker couldn't tolerate them any longer and swung round
to beg Cluff for action, anything to relieve him from this
spectacle, which was unmanning him as much as Fairchild was
unmanned already. He gaped, like an idiot, unable to credit
the evidence of his eyes. The Sergeant wasn't there: the dog
wasn't there: he and Fairchild had the room to themselves.

Did he shut the back door when he ran out? He couldn't
remember as he peered either way along the cinder path. The
Duty Constable had gone into his house and nothing human
moved in any direction.

He hurried as fast as he could go, round the corner between

this row and its neighbour, into the road. In the light cast by the lamps he caught sight of Clive and Cluff going towards Gunnarshaw and when he overtook them he couldn't speak until he'd taken time to recover his breath. Trotting by the Sergeant's side, grasping his sleeve, he protested, "We can't leave him in that state."

Cluff halted. The headlights of a passing car bathed him in a white glow, making Clive wince and slink farther away from the kerb. "Where were you?" Barker asked. "Where were you between the time you left me by the office he works in and the time you found me outside Fairchild's?" He didn't wait for a reply. "It was Rigsby," he said. "She was having an affair with Rigsby."

"What of it?"

"Her husband had found out."

They approached the centre of the town, past the cinema, from which the strains of music came faintly, the lamps shining like daylight, and they could smell frying from a fish-and-chip shop. Through the windows of a coffee-bar teenagers had theirs heads close together against the background of a wall painted with Spanish dancers.

"I'm going home," Cluff said, with a finality against which it was useless to argue. His arm pointed to a side alley: "That's your way," and he left Barker marooned on the corner, marching off without once turning his head, though his dog looked back on occasion for as long as Barker had them in view.

The Sergeant took his usual way, up the High Street, round the corner by the church at its top, straight on, past the junction that led to the secondary school, straight on again when he came to the next fork, instead of to the right up the road he'd driven on in the morning, back along which he'd walked with Barker after midday. The detached and semi-detached houses belonging to the town's upper class reared in their gardens on either side of him as he climbed the long hill to the crossroads at the top. The last avenue branched off to his left, a lane to his right, the houses as yet encroaching only on its nearer side. They ended here and in front of him the road that would bring him finally to his cottage plunged into the dark between the blacker bands of the hedges.

"Caleb," and Mole blocked his way, glancing askance at the dog, which growled and then remained silent, watching the Inspector alertly.

"I waited at the station," Mole explained. "I waited until dark. I rang up the cottage: I couldn't get an answer. I looked for you in the High Street." He paused. "I met Lodge there," he added. "He told me you'd been at the school too."

"Let me go," Cluff said, trying to free his arm. "I'm tired."

"Not this time." The Inspector dragged him towards the mouth of the avenue, surprised not to meet with a greater resistance, still wary of the dog, along to the gate of his own house. "Come in," he begged, the Sergeant's weight all at once too much for him.

"It's still empty," Cluff said, peering at the house in the next block where Bright Culter had lived and Hilda Blackoe had met her death.* Could he remember a "For Sale" notice on a post in the front garden that wasn't there any more? Was the Inspector saying, "Someone's taken it. They took the sign down yesterday. With all this going on I haven't had time to

* *The Blindness of Sergeant Cluff*

find out who"? "But I know," the Sergeant thought, and he was sure of it, this the place to which Fairchild had been going to bring his wife. In a way it had begun here, Culter leading him to the mill, what had happened at the mill resulting in the invitation to him to present the prizes at the school, back full circle to Rigsby, whose lighted windows he could see in the distance, past Mole's gable, over the garden where the schoolmaster had found one morning not long ago a dead body lying in the rain.

Mole looked across the intervening space at Rigsby's as well. "We've lived back to back all these years," he said, "and I never suspected."

His wife's head appeared from the living-room door as they came into the hall and withdrew after one look at their faces. The Inspector pushed the Sergeant into a sitting-room and put on the lights and drew the curtains before he clicked the switch of an electric fire. He said, "Didn't Rigsby give himself away to you too?"

"He's lost something."

"You're joking! Will you tell me next he was in love with her? A man of his age! Where was she killed? Who did the hut belong to?"

"Why?"

"Can't you think of a dozen reasons?"

"Is that what you wanted to talk about?"

"He's our man. It was written all over him."

"And you brought me here to tell me that!"

"Think! Think of the opportunities he had with her, working together, that study of his at the school, the access he's got to the place, at odd hours when the rest of the staff's left—" The Inspector darted after Cluff, who was already on his way back to the door: "What are you going to do about it?"

"You've no proof."

The Inspector flushed: "If you won't get it, I will."

"Good luck to you," Cluff, in the hall, said bitterly, and walked out of the front door without a word to Mrs Mole, who had reappeared. The Inspector swung slowly round to his wife and she bit off the reproaches she was about to make because he'd let the Sergeant go. "You can't do a thing with him," Mole ground out, through clenched teeth. "Not when he's in a mood like that. You'd have thought he'd have learnt his lesson. He blundered about Bright Culter and it could have cost him his life. I'm a fool for lifting a finger to help him. If he wants to ruin himself why should I stop him?"

They heard the slam of their gate and Cluff was walking, not back to the crossroads but in the other direction, round the perimeter of the square of houses with their gardens in the middle. A right-angled turn brought him to another corner, a second and similar turn to the fronts of the houses that included Rigsby's. Had his refusal to be convinced by the Inspector been pretence? Did he place so much reliance on the fact that Fairchild couldn't have driven his wife's car to where it was found? If her husband had carried her to the pool had he to carry her, in addition, along the road? If she'd gone with him willingly why had she left the car so far away? What of Fairchild's house, what of Fairchild as he and Barker had seen him so short a time ago?

Was it Rigsby he was interested in, there outside the teacher's house? Was it so easy to forget the caretaker at the school, the hint of unexpressed meaning in Lodge's attitude, the deputy headmaster's acceptance of a rival in a post he'd been expected to fill and must have hoped for himself, as he'd practically admitted? The Sergeant crossed to the opposite side of the road and stood with Clive in the shelter of a tall yew hedge, staring across the avenue. He thought of Rigsby's wife and so many people had to suffer for the actions of one of them. He knew as soon as he heard the footsteps, dragging but lighter than a man's, why he was here. She came into view under the street-lamps, slumped, lost, a girl without purpose, walking in a dream. What had troubled him most all day, what still troubled him, was her breakdown in the High Street this morning, which had sent him to the bank where she worked, which had sent him to the school to see her father. It could fit, if he made it fit, and any solution would be preferable to this one, anything to this transfer of guilt, to this harrying of the innocent, this breaking of faith, this destruction of an ideal.

She turned into her father's garden. He saw the door open and close as she disappeared into the dark interior of Rigsby's house, and age had its defences, however weak, against disillusion but youth had none.

The approach of a new figure, slinking quietly on rubber-soled feet, almost took him unawares. His head went down in warning to the dog and he pressed closer against the hedge.

He put out his arm and grasped the newcomer's sleeve, staring into the face of the clerk who worked next to her in the bank. "Why are you following her?"

"I'm not doing any wrong," and Stockwell struggled with him.

"Let me be the judge," the Sergeant said. "If I want to take you in I can think of a dozen excuses."

The youth trembled: "You can't!"

"What would it mean? Your position at the bank, Janet working there too—"

"She'll have nothing to do with me."

"That makes it worse."

"Can't you understand? – she's not herself. I'm afraid for her."

"You too?"

"She hasn't been home till now. She's been wandering all evening. I could see when we closed—"

"What would you do for her?"

"Anything, Mr Cluff."

"Her father?"

"I hate him," Stockwell said violently. "No one else exists for her. It isn't natural. What has he done to her?"

"It'll be harder than you know," and the Sergeant snapped his fingers at Clive.

Stockwell trailed them to another corner: "Then you won't say anything?"

"Won't your parents be worried about you?" and the Sergeant paced off on his way at last, leaving Gunnarshaw behind for today.

CHAPTER X

H er husband didn't move. She knew he'd scarcely stirred all night and she knew, too, that he hadn't slept, lying stiffly in the dark with those few inches of space between them that had been for so many months an insurmountable barrier to intimacy, either of the mind or of the flesh.

A wan daylight percolated, grey and sad, through the drawn curtains, blurring the outlines of the furniture in the room, raising a black sheen on the dressing-table mirror. She wanted to talk to him and she couldn't begin, contact lost, no possibility of bridging the gap that had grown ever wider.

Ruth Rigsby slipped from under the covers without throwing them back, the chill pile of the bedside rug striking at her bare feet, and her body, in its nightdress, shivered. Whose fault? Was a woman in her forties, with a daughter almost grown up, old?

She reached for her corset, left neatly with her other clothing on a chair, and pulled it up under the nightdress. Her knickers followed and she had her back to the bed before she let the nightdress drop from her shoulders, hiding her breasts from view during that brief moment before she covered them, an expert in the art of clothing herself without revealing her body, just as she was at night in undressing, with him lying there waiting. Had he ever seen her nude? What sin of unnatural modesty had she committed during these twenty years of marriage? She could remember the look in his eyes in those early days, the hurt disappointment, his gaze as she turned away from him. He'd wanted her naked in his arms and naked in his sight and she couldn't, the shame of showing herself to him that had afflicted her on their marriage-night become a habit she hadn't been able to break. He'd hoped, pleading silently from the bed, until he'd ceased to hope and withdrawn from her, the intervals growing longer and longer, the barriers higher. She'd allowed him love, in the dark, decently shrouded and covered, passive under his fumblings, but when had she felt it herself in the manner he'd expected, when had she responded with the passion to which he considered himself entitled, when, now that she thought of it, had their lips met as their flesh became one? Not his fault, hers, and a fault too long-standing, too ingrained, ever to be remedied at this late stage of their marital life. Could she be blamed for what she was, the attitudes she'd learnt as a child in her parents' house, the repressions exercised on her during adolescence by a god-fearing mother and a strict father? She'd been faithful, kind in her duties in everything except this, running her home in a model fashion, caring for him, tacitly supporting his ambitions, leaving to him the major decisions of their mutual existence. She'd made no complaints, following him where he went, but had they ever been really in love? What was love? Why could they not interpret its meaning alike? Did it have to be different for her and for him?

She opened their door quietly and went out on to the landing, pausing to listen outside Janet's room, this house a house of quiet, a widening gulf between them all. They seemed hardly to talk with each other any more, as if they'd exhausted all their subjects of conversation, nothing left to say, everything said already. She had her hand on the handle of the door, her fingers gripping to turn it, but she'd never been one with her daughter and her husband. Had he sought in the child a compensation for his deprivations only to discover, as she grew into a woman, that their relationship was false, doomed because of the division between the generations? If he had been Svengali could Janet continue for ever to be Trilby?

The morning newspaper rattled through the letter-flap and dropped with a tiny thud to the floor as she descended the stairs into the hall. She picked it up on her way to the kitchen and put it on the table while she began the first tasks of her day, drawing back the curtains, opening the damper of the all-night-burning fire, pulling out the ash-pan to empty it. He was moving upstairs, unusually early, and she pricked her ears for the wail of the buzz at the mill by which Gunnarshaw set its clocks, doubtful of the time shown by that on the mantelpiece.

She had the table laid for breakfast, bacon frying in the pan, the kettle on the boil, her activities punctuated by the running of the bathroom taps, before he appeared, shaved and dressed, pale-faced, his eyes undershadowed, not like himself, almost a stranger, his walk jerky, an unsteadiness about him, lacking that air of authority his work had fostered increasingly as he grew older. Bent over the gas-jets on top of the cooker, she watched him grope for the newspaper, still in its folds, by his plate. The pages rustled as he turned them and she held her breath because he was holding his. The egg she cracked on the edge of the frying-pan almost disintegrated under the force of the blow and voided in a mess of running yolk into the spluttering fat.

He toyed with his food, compelling himself to eat, and she could see that every mouthful nearly choked him. The newspaper lay crumpled and unread, hastily and inexpertly refolded, under the guard of his elbow. His eyes stared across the table and saw nothing. He fidgeted and she thought a number of times he was going to get up but on each occasion he collapsed back into his chair. The chiming clock in the sitting-room struck the hour and he asked, mumbling the words, "Isn't she coming down?"

"I'll call her," Ruth replied, and he was on his feet at once, before her into the hall, reaching for his hat, stopping in mid-motion in the act of taking down his coat from its hook. He dashed back into the kitchen to reappear with the newspaper crushed in his fist.

"You're going so early," she said, "even before she's up?" He had his coat on already and was turning back the lock on the front door. "You're not taking the car?" Its keys lay on the hall-table, where they were always left, and they hypnotized her, there all yesterday too. He'd never walked before these two days and he'd always made a point of arriving after the rest of his staff, leaving the donkey-work to Lodge, appearing only in time to take morning prayers in the hall, when they were all assembled and waiting.

The door closed behind him and the keys remained on the table. "Janet!" she shouted from the foot of the stairs, and started up slowly: "Janet!" She repeated, "Janet!" again, her tone filled with concern, when she entered her daughter's room, walking rapidly to the bed and putting a hand on the girl's brow: "You're ill." The skin burnt beneath her touch and the eyes looking up at her were fevered. "Have you been awake all night?" She laid her head closer in a vain attempt to make sense of her daughter's reply: "Shall I send for the doctor?" The violence of the reaction shocked her. She said, "But you can't go to work," and her heart sank. "Where were you last night? What happened to make you so late?"

"I heard the front door."

"He's gone."

The girl shifted on to her side, her face to the wall, but she couldn't hide her tears from her mother, who asked, afraid, "Is there anything you want to confide? Can't I help?" The futility of the question struck her before she'd completed it and it wasn't her to whom her daughter turned, or had ever turned, but to her husband.

"Stay where you are," Mrs Rigsby said. "I'll ring the bank."

"I can't go back! I can't ever go back!"

"But what have you done?" and the mother clutched at the daughter, pulling her round.

The nightdress tore at the neck, exposing firm, young breasts, as Janet wrenched from her hold. "Go away!" and the girl's voice broke. "Leave me alone!" It recovered and grew shrill. "Leave me alone! Leave me alone! Leave me alone!"

"Tell me! What is it? What's happened?" She tried again to pull her daughter to her and for a moment they struggled together in actual conflict, until the strength went out of the elder woman. Did it matter? Did anything matter?

"I'll bring you something to eat," Ruth tried. "We'll talk about it when your father comes home."

"I hate him!" the girl said, repeating Stockwell's words to Cluff last night, making her mother recoil.

How could she work? How did she dare so much as to move, a prey to nameless terrors, listening for those sounds from her daughter's bedroom, certain that the tray she'd taken up remained untouched? She crept backwards and forwards between the kitchen and the foot of the stairs, drawn as much by the keys on the hall-table as by her inadequacy to give comfort, until she couldn't stand it any longer. She rushed outside to the garage built on to the gable of the house but she couldn't get in. None of the keys on the ring fitted, though the one she wanted should have been there.

In the house again she searched everywhere, on the mantelpieces, in the drawers of the kitchen table, in those of the desk he used, though not so frequently these days, when he brought work home from the school, looking in all the places where the garage key had never been. In the end she took a hammer and chisel from the toolbox in the coalplace and forced the lock, careless of what the neighbours might think or see.

Her heart pumped furiously and she couldn't catch her breath. She clutched at her breast with her hand, trembling, nothing amiss, unable to believe it. The daylight flooded in through the double doors she'd swung widely back: the radiator grille leered at her, the car parked with its bonnet to the entrance: the bicycle Janet had used for school before she started at the bank leaned against the rear wall. "Mrs Rigsby," a voice said from behind her.

The hand at her breast jerked to her lips. "Did I startle you?" the voice asked, and when she shook her head it wouldn't stop shaking.

"I saw him leave," Inspector Mole said, looking at the broken lock. "Have you lost the key?" He smiled. "I was at the school yesterday. He wasn't using the car then either." He waited a moment. "Did you come home in it together from speech-day? Was that when you lost the key?"

"He'd some work to do. I walked back," and she could have bitten off her tongue.

"You've been in the country?" the Inspector said, his eyes on the tyres of the car.

"What do you mean?"

"My wife too. She complains as well when I can't get home. Sometimes I'm out till the small hours."

"He's never as late as that."

"The night before last?"

"I must go in."

"Or any night?"

"He's a lot to do, not only for the school—"

"I know what it is to be short of staff. It'll be more difficult until he finds a replacement for Mrs Fairchild. We're even in the national press this morning, I see. Did you know her well?" She grabbed at the door jamb, her knees weak, and a hint of crocodile tears sounded in the Inspector's voice. "A pity I didn't pass a moment or two earlier. Perhaps I could have opened it for you without breaking it."

When he'd gone she dared to look at the car more closely and saw the mud dried on the tyres and spotting the coachwork. She ran back into the hall and called up the stairs: "I'm going out for a few minutes. I shan't be long."

CHAPTER XI

"You didn't arrest Fairchild," the Duty Constable said, as Barker walked into the police station, a statement rather than an accusation. "Dolly wouldn't have thanked you if you had."

"You've seen inside his house?"

"I've heard people talk about it."

"They can't pay him much at his office."

"They pay plenty: it comes out of your pocket and mine."

"But money doesn't go far."

"You're asking me or telling me?"

"The Sergeant?"

"Let him take his own time," and the constable followed Barker's glance to the telephone on the counter.

"I'm supposed to have a job here," Barker said.

"The Inspector's not in either."

"Can't he keep his nose out of it?"

"The pot calling the kettle black?"

"Does Patterson at Headquarters know?"

"Not from anybody here but he will by now if he reads the newspapers."

Barker went back to the street again. He looked for Cluff in the High Street without success and perhaps the abrupt manner in which the Sergeant had left him the evening before rankled a little. "What would I do," he thought, "if the woman I'd married, the woman on whom I'd lavished everything, started going with other men?" and he wouldn't have succumbed himself to Mrs Fairchild's wiles. On the stroke of nine he made for her husband's office and twenty minutes later he'd seen, outside, no sign of the man he was looking for. He climbed the stairs but Fairchild hadn't had the advantage of him. How could he be there, with his wife dead?

He stood in the corridor, listening to the excited conversation, feeling the tension in the air, and they'd read their papers. In the end he sought an interview with the manager, a mousy little man with a high opinion of himself which seemed at the moment somewhat the worse for wear. Briefly annoyed at being fobbed off with a junior, the man said, "I expected Sergeant Cluff," but his nervousness soon came back and his fingers tapped continually on the top of his desk.

"You've given Fairchild leave?" Barker asked.

"It's not an hour ago since I saw it in the press!" The fingers tapped harder. "I'd rather have discussed this with Cluff."

"He handled money?"

"What has he confessed to?"

Both pairs of eyes turned to a pile of ledgers on the manager's desk. "His?" Barker said.

"I've just had them brought in."

"It could have been going on for a long time."

"Haven't I a right to trust my employees?" The manager's voice quietened and he added, pathetically: "Nothing like this has ever happened to me before."

Barker laid a hand on the top ledger: "His wife couldn't pay for everything. Hadn't he just bought a new house too? You'll have to let us know when you've been through his books in detail."

"He killed her, didn't he?" and Barker said nothing. "Didn't he?" the manager repeated. "It's an open secret she despised him."

"Then he'll hardly be concerned about mere embezzlement."

The manager jumped to his feet as if he was going to stop Barker leaving the office and suddenly realized there was nothing he could do. He called, "Mind you, I never cottoned on to him. I inherited him when I took over this post—"

"Is that all you're worried about?" Barker thought, as he shut the door. "What's going to happen to you if he's been stealing?"

He went down the stairs and along the High Street but there was still no sign of the Sergeant. In the telephone kiosk in front of the Town Hall he pressed Button A when he heard Annie Croft's voice and said, "It's Barker."

"Hold on," and in the cottage Annie put the receiver down and ran to the porch. She shouted after Cluff, who was going along the garden path with Clive, and panted up with her message when he waited. He told her, "Tell him I've gone," and walked off.

She'd no alternative but to say so when she got back to the phone and she asked, "Does he know already who it is?"

"Where to?" Barker demanded.

"He looks as if his mind's made up."

"How long ago?"

She stretched a point: "A few minutes," and the line went dead. She replaced the receiver and went back to the porch but she could see nothing of Cluff, who was already out of sight, swinging quickly towards Gunnarshaw. He passed the end of Mole's avenue but, instead of going on into the town, he turned along the next, down which Rigsby lived, driving himself on against his will.

A light, intermittent breeze played with the unfastened doors of the headmaster's garage and when he got to it the drive outside the threshold was damp. Clive, sensitive to his mood, stayed at his heels as he studied the patches of wet on the concrete floor near the tyres. The paintwork of the car closest to the ground had a dull bloom, washed but not polished, contrasting with the shinier portions round the windows and on top of the bonnet. The woman's cycle at the back of the garage interested him more and he squeezed between the wall and the car to examine it. Rusty, its saddle cracked, the brakes worked when he tested them and its tyres were reasonably hard.

He sighed and, if he hadn't noticed the curtains at an upstairs window of the house flutter, he might still have gone away instead of walking to the front door and ringing its bell.

The dog entered with him, though neither he nor Mrs Rigsby paid it the slightest attention. She was about to take him into the sitting-room but he looked down at his boots, shaking his head, and passed her, out of the hall, along the passage by the side of the stairs, to the kitchen. A bucket on the draining board of the sink, with a wash-leather over its rim, leapt to his eye. He walked to three newspapers, all open at accounts of Mrs Fairchild's death, spread on the table and said, "Do you take all these?" She stared at him, disturbed, and he asked, "Or have you been down to the newsagent's on the main road to buy them yourself?"

He ran his eyes over the relevant columns: "They haven't missed much out." In one of them the reporter had been acute, stealing a march on the others, emphasizing, though only as a coincidence, that the body of the murdered woman had been discovered in the vicinity of a weekend hut belonging to the man under whom she worked, leaving his readers to make of it what they would.

He supported Mrs Rigsby to a chair at the table, where she slumped with her head bowed. He sought for words but he couldn't find any and he hated himself and his position, and people.

"We'd grown apart," she said at last, breaking the silence between them. "Wasn't it apparent when you had tea with us at the school?"

He hardly trusted himself to speak: "You've been cleaning the car."

"I told the Inspector – He stayed at school after the prize-giving finished – to work. She'd gone before I left. I watched her leave."

"You weren't with him all the time that afternoon."

"I'd people to talk to, the arrangements for tea to supervise."

"Janet hasn't gone to work today," he said. "I saw her at the bedroom window."

"She's not well."

After a long pause, he asked, "Can she drive?"

"Of course. But why?"

"I saw her last night as well. It was late."

"I can't keep her tied to my apron-strings."

"Not only last night," he said, despising himself for the lie.

"The night before too. Once or twice on other occasions."

"She's a good girl—"

"And close to her father."

"Don't!" and the door bell, ringing loudly, interrupted them. It startled them both and made Clive growl. "Answer it," Cluff said.

He moved to the kitchen door, silently, when she'd left the room, opening it a little way, standing behind it and listening. He heard Lodge's voice saying, "I had to go to the bank to pay in some dinner-money. Janet wasn't there."

"Haven't you put enough ideas into her head as it is?" Mrs Rigsby asked.

The deputy headmaster spoke quietly: "Was I mistaken?"

"After you'd posed as our friend!"

"Ruth—"

She began to close the door in his face: "Please go."

"His career was at stake," Lodge said. "She'd have bled him dry. I could only hint, to try to prepare you—"

"Me?" she told him, scornfully. "Or Janet, who's young enough to be your daughter, or your granddaughter?"

"You're doing me an injustice," Lodge began, but the door cut off the rest of his words and when Mrs Rigsby returned to the kitchen the Sergeant was by the table as she'd left him.

"Why my husband?" she demanded. "Was he the only one? Hasn't she a husband too?" but he walked by her into the passage.

At the foot of the stairs he glanced up in time to see a flurry of white disappear on the landing and Mrs Rigsby saw it too. He wanted to go up there and he ought to have done but he couldn't. Nevertheless, it was hard to make up his mind

and he leaned heavily on the newel post, miserable, for a long
time before he said at last, "I shall have to come back."

"Here?"

"When your husband's at home."

"Can't you see him at the school?"

"It isn't that."

CHAPTER XII

Barker walked up the hill from the town without seeing Cluff and Clive approaching. His pace slackened and he went more and more slowly until he stopped altogether, unable to forget Fairchild, that cold house and that broken man in the midst of the luxury he'd created for a wife who'd never loved him. The memory of the empty desk in the lax, excited office haunted him and he couldn't rid himself of a picture in his mind of figures on the pages of an accounts book. He stared up the empty road but nothing moved and nothing came by him from behind, neither pedestrians nor cars.

Abruptly, he turned on his heels. His progress down the High Street attracted the stares of the passers-by and comments from the women he jostled. A double-decked red bus drove out of the bus station on the opposite side of the road as he passed the cinema and he jumped for the rear platform, missing his footing, grabbing the hand-rail, dragged along faster and faster. The conductor leaned over and seized him by the shoulder to pull him on board. "If you want to kill yourself," he said, "don't do it when I'm about." He recognized Barker. "All this trouble and if I ask you for a fare I'll probably get myself arrested into the bargain. I've done nowt," – he glanced at his few passengers – "and this lot doesn't look capable of it. If it's the driver you're after we'll all have to hoof it."

"I'm not going far."

"I'll stop it for you," the conductor said. "You've taken enough risks for one day," and adopted a wise expression. "That woman you found yesterday?"

The houses ended and began again and the conductor rang his bell between stops to let Barker off, exactly opposite Fairchild's house. "Right to the door," he remarked. "Did he get rid of his old woman himself? Give him my address if another or two won't make any difference to him. He can't have suffered more than I do."

From the front the house showed no sign of occupation but then, none of them in the row did, the windows dead-eyed and the rooms behind them lifeless. On the cinder path at their backs he ducked under a line of washing suspended between a hook in the wall of the Duty Constable's ash-pit and a clothes-post by the fence separating the path from the field. He hesitated before opening Fairchild's gate but only for a moment, crossing the yard to knock loudly on the back door. His heart came into his mouth and the blind, still lowered over the living-room window, prevented him from seeing inside.

It occurred to him only slowly to lift the sneck and the door yielded so suddenly and unexpectedly that he nearly pitched full length across the threshold. He hardly had courage to turn into the living-room and the instant he did so he was certain that his fears had been justified.

In what daylight penetrated he saw Fairchild sitting in the upholstered armchair on the other side of the fireplace, almost lost in its vastness, his hands splayed, palms down and very thin, on the arms. He stared at Barker with unblinking eyes, quite still, his face dead white except for a hint of shadow round his jowls and on his upper lip, looking so peaceful that death might have come naturally, no wound or blood visible. The ashes of yesterday's apology for a fire lay sparse in the grate, the same pots and loaf of bread and jar of jam the detective-constable had seen the night before on the table.

"I wasn't brave enough," the corpse said, only its lips moving, and Barker nearly jumped out of his skin. His eyes rounded in disbelief and the voice added, "I've never been brave: she often told me so."

What could he say – "You're alive?" or, "You've been here all night," or, "You'd have gone on sitting in that chair for ever if I hadn't walked in."? All true, all equally unnecessary. He moistened his lips with his tongue, replying, "They expected to hear from you at the office," and went to wind up the blind.

"Don't they know?" Fairchild said.

"Everyone knows."

"And thinks I killed her?"

"Perhaps."

"They never credited me with anything before."

"You ought to have something to eat," and the farthest thought from Barker's mind had been to act as butler to a murderer. He made tea on the cooker in the scullery and opened a tin of chicken breasts from a pantry well-stocked with expensive items. Fairchild cleaned his plate and drank his tea without protest.

"They're checking your books," Barker said.

"I imagined they would if ever my back was turned. I didn't dare to take a holiday last year. My wife went away on her own."

"How much?"

A suspicion of a smile played on Fairchild's lips: "A lot –
I've lost count," and he saw the pity in Barker's face. "I didn't
expect it to go on as long as it has done. She'd have left me, of
course, as soon as they found out."

"Then why?" Barker asked, astonished.

"It kept her with me for the time being."

"But you realized it was coming to an end?"

"Copying signatures on cheques or amending figures isn't
hard: it was easy to juggle with the books. I didn't know I
could do it till I tried. Sometimes I planned one last coup, so
that we could have gone away together, abroad, somewhere
they'd never catch up with me, but I'd have had to tell her
about it and she wouldn't have come along."

"I'm taking you to the station."

"Anything's preferable to sitting here."

They washed and dried the dishes and put them in the
cupboard. Barker said, "I'll turn the water off, and the gas and
the electricity, if you'll tell me where to look."

"You're a careful man," Fairchild replied. "I thought all
night about putting a match to it but people live on both
sides."

"We'll lock up at the back from the inside and go out at the
front. The outhouses in the yard?"

"There's hardly anything in there," and when they were in
the road Fairchild paused to look back: "I've often wondered
who would get it."

"You've no heirs?"

"Not a single relative. Will they sell it to repay part of what
I've stolen?"

"I couldn't say. The Sergeant might know."

"I rather hope not. I've never liked the people in that office."

Barker took him by the arm and led him across the road to scramble up the steep bank on to the canal towpath: "We shan't meet anyone this way."

"You're not ashamed to be seen in my company?"

"It's pleasanter by the water."

The towpath brought them almost to the centre of the town and Barker avoided the main streets when they left it, taking Fairchild along alleys and through passages, up and down flights of steps in hillsides. His prisoner walked jauntily and they arrived at the police station and entered the outer office without incident.

The Duty Constable's eyes popped when he saw them. Inspector Mole, pacing the floor like a caged lion, bubbling with frustration and anger, his face very red, his movements rapid, failed for a moment to notice them but the expression on the constable's face warned him of something untoward and he stared too.

"I've brought him in," Barker said. "He didn't give any trouble," and looked for a chair for Fairchild: "Perhaps you'd like to sit down?"

The Inspector found his tongue: "You've gone daft?" and slapped a hand against his forehead. "Is everyone crazy?" His visions of a personal triumph began to dim and he turned on Barker: "He didn't do it. I don't have to tolerate nonsense like this. Who gave you a licence to interfere? God knows I never considered you very brilliant when you were in the uniformed branch but this is too much."

"We all make mistakes," Cluff said, from the frame of the
street door, "even you, Inspector," and Clive came forward
from beside him, his tail wagging, to nuzzle Fairchild's hand,
as he had done Abbie's at Cracknell's cottage.

"Rigsby'll get away," Mole protested. "You'll be lucky if he's
not gone already," and he glared at Fairchild with hostility.
"This madman can't alter facts. What can't speak can't lie."

"I'm an embezzler too," Fairchild confessed happily. "I've
stolen hundreds of pounds." Mole's face fell. "It was all for
nothing. I didn't think she was on her own when she went out
at nights. She always aimed for the top. It had to be Rigsby.
I've been to his hut and seen them there."

The Inspector made an effort. "He stood by and let you kill
her, I suppose?" he asked, sarcastically. "Did he carry her up to
the pool for you afterwards?"

"She'd have a key," Cluff said. "They wouldn't go together
when they met at the hut: Gunnarshaw has too many eyes."
He regarded Mole steadily: "I haven't seen what was in her
handbag: you have."

"Very well," and the Inspector dug in his pocket and threw
a key on the counter. "I was going to tell you. Must I spell
it out for you? If you'd followed even the most elementary
rules—" His pupils rolled in silent appeal to the deity. "Rigsby
stayed behind at the school – an excuse; he'll never be able to
prove it. They'd arranged a meeting for later—"

"The mud on his car wheels?"

"So you haven't been wasting your time altogether?"

"It isn't there any more. His wife's washed it off."

"What! Never mind. He still followed her out there."

"Why not? – he was her lover."

"Ah! You've found that out, have you?"

"You didn't talk to the caretaker at the school?"

"I'd have got around to it."

"Then he didn't have to kill her."

"Good God, man, an affair like that doesn't last! Look at his position, his standing in the town. He's a wife and family. He'd got himself into a jam and she wouldn't let him go." His eyes went to Fairchild. "Ask him to tell you what sort of a woman she was."

"And her car, half a mile down the road?"

"You're not that much of a fool. He went in his and he could hardly leave her body in the hut – I take it you'll allow me that much? He took it up to the pool, where it might never have been discovered. But her car was there and so was his. How much time had he to play about with? He couldn't cope with both at once. He got in hers and drove it off as far as he dared – gloves on his hands, of course – but he had to get home in case anyone started asking questions and he had to walk back to get his own car, where he'd left it parked at the mouth of that track leading to the ghyll. He couldn't take all night."

The Sergeant looked at Fairchild: "It's the only explanation for the car," he said, "and you don't drive. If you could you'd nothing to go back for and you needn't have left the car as close as it was to the spot."

"We're getting somewhere," the Inspector interrupted, with satisfaction. "Well, what are we waiting for?" The others stood still. "Is nobody prepared to go and get Rigsby?" and he started for the street door. Janet collided with him as he was going through and he turned, his face a study in conflicting emotions, to watch her walk to the counter, on which she placed a creased, silky scarf.

"Don't listen to her," Fairchild begged.

Barker's heart sank and he wondered, until Cluff broke the silence, whether any of them was ever going to speak again. "Because she's young?" the Sergeant said to Fairchild. "Because she has her life to live?" An eternity passed before he added, "How could she be happy with a secret like that? She's no hardened criminal. She has a conscience. There'd be no surer way of damning her."

CHAPTER XIII

"At least," Fairchild pleaded, "lock me up."

The Duty Constable dragged his eyes from the door of the C.I.D. room, which was just closing, and only the two of them remained in the outer office.

"I could insist I did it," Fairchild proposed. "Why should they believe Janet Rigsby more than they believe me?"

"It isn't any good," the constable replied. "You can only guess what happened. She knows."

"They'll treat her leniently?"

"If Caleb has anything to do with it. Don't take on. Even judges have a habit of listening to him when he's in the witness box." He lifted the flap in the counter and walked to the street door to close it. The sunlight coming in through the window mocked him and, if he'd had his way, he'd have drawn the blind as well. But he wasn't even quick enough with the door or successful in preventing Lodge's entry.

"Where is she?" the deputy headmaster demanded breathlessly, and started for the C.I.D. room without waiting for a reply. The constable stepped in front of him and said, "No!" and asked, "Why aren't you at school?"

"Let me go!"

"You followed her."

"I'm a friend of the family."

"They'll need friends."

"What has she said?"

"It's our affair."

"I did my best," Fairchild interrupted, and Lodge noticed him for the first time. "They won't listen."

Lodge's voice rose: "But her father killed your wife."

"It's all finished," the constable said, and Lodge tottered. "Let me get you a glass of water."

"Janet's lying!"

"You'd better rest a while."

"I ought to have killed her," Fairchild murmured.

They watched Lodge stumble blindly out of the office for the street and the constable went to the C.I.D. room door. He lifted his hand and rapped on the frosted-glass panel. The door opened and he saw, over Barker's shoulder, Janet Rigsby's back, the girl facing Cluff across his table, the Sergeant's eyes fixed on the tattered blotting-pad. Mole stood despondently by the window.

"What is it?" Barker asked.

"Nothing," the Duty Constable replied.

Barker closed the door and stood with his back to it: nobody in the room seemed to have noticed the interruption.

"I saw you," the Sergeant said to Janet, "crying in the High Street. We met that afternoon in the bank. You saw me from your bedroom window this morning. You listened on the landing when I was talking to your mother. Last night you wandered the town, too distressed to go home." His fingers played idly with the scarf she'd brought. "You heard what Lodge said, too, when he came to your door."

"They all thought it was my father."

"I never thought so: I knew you loved him." He watched the tears roll down her cheeks. "Shall I send for him?"

Her face crumpled more and the Sergeant got to his feet and Clive came out from under the table: "Your mother will have to know."

"I can't see him," she said. "I won't see him!"

Cluff walked to the door and nodded to Barker, who opened it for him. The Inspector hesitated and then followed into the outer office, leaving the detective-constable and the girl in the room. He ignored the presence of the Duty Constable and Fairchild and bearded the Sergeant: "She's trying to protect him."

"And the scarf?"

"A young girl!"

"Mrs Fairchild would have left the hut door open for Rigsby. Janet had only to come up behind her."

"She couldn't have carried her to the pool!"

"What aren't we capable of – any of us – in moments of crisis?"

"That car!"

"Did you miss the bicycle at the back of the garage? What you said about the reason for the car being where we found it applies equally to the girl. She had to go back for the cycle." The Sergeant ordered the Duty Constable: "Phone her mother!"

The dial of the telephone whirred softly: they listened to the constable's voice and the vague reply, indistinguishable, at the other end of the line, telling them by its tone what effect the message had. "Janet loved him too much," Cluff said. "Is it hard to imagine how she felt when she learnt he'd gone elsewhere, to another woman, a woman already married? She had to win him back, to save him from himself." His voice trailed away and then strengthened. "I think perhaps Abbie Cracknell saw her."

"She's said so?" the Inspector asked.

"It was what she left unsaid. What odds does it make? Janet knew what Rigsby was using the hut for. She knew when Mrs. Fairchild drove off and her father stayed behind at the school they were going to meet later, and where. How long would it take her to cycle there? Something kept Rigsby and when he arrived the hut was empty. You've seen him since and I've seen him and if she'd moved the car to the lay-by already he couldn't have missed it. But what could he do, involved as he was? Mrs Fairchild wasn't at the hut: she didn't arrive at the school next day. He suspected what I suspected at least, maybe with more cause than I had and there must have been quarrels between him and his daughter."

Fairchild started for the corridor leading to the back of the police station and the Duty Constable hurried after him. "He won't run away," Cluff said. "You don't even have to turn a key on him."

The constable didn't return and the Sergeant wished that he, too, could have hidden himself somewhere, anywhere so long as he didn't have to face Mrs. Rigsby. His eyes and Mole's both fastened on the outer door but, when she came, it wasn't as bad as they'd thought. Instead of hysterics she was composed, and had she feared this and prepared herself for it, aware that Janet hadn't been at home that evening? She said, "I don't know how she got out of the house to come here: I thought she was in her bedroom," and Cluff took her hand

and led her to the C.I.D. room. He called Barker out and they stood together by the counter, with the Inspector, unable to hear anything of what was going on between the woman and the girl.

CHAPTER XIV

Barker sat in a chair, stroking Clive's head, both the man and the dog glancing surreptitiously from time to time at Cluff, still leaning on the counter. The Inspector, unable to keep entirely still, paced a few steps occasionally and then came to a halt. They'd formalities to complete, statements to record, charges to swear, warrants to have signed, an appearance before the magistrates to arrange. The fingers of the clock on the wall dragged their dilatory course and none of them showed any eagerness to set the wheels in motion or to bring this out into the open. When the C.I.D. room door opened at last Mole fled hastily to his own office and Mrs Rigsby started for the street without speaking. Cluff overtook her and said, "Your husband needs your support. You need him."

"After what he's done?"

"He couldn't have foreseen it."

"Not to me. To her."

He let her go and Janet still huddled on the chair in front of his table. The Duty Constable reappeared at last from the rear of the station, without Fairchild, and Inspector Mole left the refuge of his office. Events moved slowly and yet time seemed to gallop, procrastination no help, this postponement of action no bar to its ultimate necessity. In some way they didn't understand each of them silently accused the other of hastening this girl to her doom. In the end one of them called a woman constable to take her away.

The Sergeant and Barker had the C.I.D. room to themselves again, Clive at Cluff's feet, the Inspector appearing and disappearing in the doorway. Once the detective-constable tried to apologize for his mistake about Fairchild but he got neither encouragement nor reproach and slipped into his thoughts again. Could he see now the man wasn't capable of murder and which could he trust, feelings or facts, or could he trust either? What kind of man did he need to be to ensure success in his calling, one cool, calculating, analytical, abstractedly material, or one passionate and sensitive, translating his own longings and fears into the guilt of others, sensing not proving the motivations behind their deeds? What was crime? Did its distinctions lie not in the pages of the statute books but in the characters of its perpetrators? Was it his misfortune or his advantage to work in Gunnarshaw, where no one seemed wholly good or wholly bad, to have to deal not with professional lawbreakers but with people?

Cluff sat back in his chair, in that customary attitude of his on these occasions, hands in pockets, chin on chest, tweed hat shadowing half-closed eyes, heavy face expressionless, lumpish. Why didn't he go home? Hadn't it been simpler this time than usual, no hunt, no chase to apprehend the quarry, no one except the victim physically hurt?

The dog under the table knew better than to disturb the quiet and Barker supposed that he did too. The ticking of their watches had a hypnotic effect, removing himself from himself, giving his surroundings a transitory, blurred, impermanent appearance. The real world receded and he existed in a dream universe, peaceful so long as he didn't move or think, the future as far away as the past and no present.

The light dimmed gradually into dusk: the Duty Constable in the outer office forced a cough: Inspector Mole reappeared in the doorway. The Sergeant looked up and muttered, "What must it be like at Rigsby's house?" Barker's brain started to function again and he thought, "If she goads her husband too far with her reproaches?" He asked himself, "Are we entirely sane? How could he have been responsible to get mixed up with Mrs Fairchild when he'd everything to lose – position, home, family, his daughter's love – and so little to win?"

"In any event," the Inspector said, "I can run you to the top of the hill."

The detective-constable found himself once more in the rear seat of the minicar, his long body jack-knifed, Clive's head on his thigh, and was it always assumed that he, like the dog, would follow? He felt no surprise when Mole turned off along the avenue before his own and drew to a stop outside Rigsby's house. By tacit agreement they stayed where they were while Cluff got out.

The clouds that had gathered to end this spell of fine weather deepened the twilight and the globes of the patented street-lamps showed a pale blue. From the car they watched the Sergeant go up the drive and ring the headmaster's doorbell. They waited for the fanlight to glow yellow and their hearts contracted little by little, a helplessness nailing them to their seats, refusing to name their fears. Her appearance at last merely increased the invisible burden weighing on them. She exchanged a few words with the Sergeant, who came back down the drive and closed the gate. He got into the car and said, "She hasn't seen him since he went out this morning. He hasn't been home all day."

They digested this for some moments and then Mole spoke for both himself and Barker: "Surely she rang him up at the school?" but were Rigsby and his wife too far apart even for that?

"Won't he at least have heard about his daughter?" Barker added.

"How can he have done unless from her? No one else left the station."

"His wife's friends?"

"She's told no one. I believe her."

The Inspector put the car into gear and for the third time in as many days Cluff passed between the ornamental gateposts towards the mass of the school, its huge expanse of glass dim now, like sightless Cyclops' eyes, the brown tint of its new stone shadowed, a blackness about the playing fields beyond that had been, earlier, so freshly green.

"They've all gone home," the Inspector said, but the figure of the caretaker, emerging from a side door and bending to lock it, gave him the lie.

Again the Sergeant got out while the others stayed in the car, listening. The caretaker straightened and said, "There's nobody here." He volunteered, "The children were let out early. There's been no work done today. Everything's been at sixes and sevens."

"Open the door," the Sergeant ordered, and Mole and Barker joined him but he told them, "Leave Clive where he is."

He knew his way about the place by now and led them, with the caretaker at the rear, up the stairs to the upper corridor. He tried the door of the headmaster's study and it resisted his pressure. "The key," he said to the caretaker.

"I haven't got one."

"Didn't he trust you after all, Elijah?"

"That wasn't the reason." The man snarled. "He wanted his privacy. He had it cleaned in the mornings when I wasn't the only one about."

The Sergeant put his shoulder to the upper panel, which split with a sharp crack. The tongue of the lock ground in its socket: wood creaked and tore. He withdrew a little before charging and the door flew open under his weight but the sight of Rigsby checked his impetus. Behind him the caretaker choked back nausea and Barker closed his eyes, the Inspector's groan ringing in his ears.

Somebody said, "Stay where you are."

The door banged, shutting Elijah out in the corridor but leaving Barker and Mole on the wrong side of it with Cluff, and they had to look. Very gradually, Barker allowed his eyes to slide to the floor in front of the fireplace and once he'd succeeded in controlling his own desire to vomit he couldn't take his gaze away. Cluff and Mole stared just as hard and fixedly.

The tiled hearth rose a few inches above floor level and the broken, bruised skin on Rigsby's temple showed how he'd hit its corner as he fell but that was only the smallest part of it, a detail they didn't take in at once. The electric fire had been overturned and the hilt and part of the blade of one of the foils from the wall above the mantelpiece were

wedged through the wire mesh of its guard, which had been
partly wrenched off. Blood soaked the hearthrug and the part
of the carpet near it, the remainder of the sword transfixing
the headmaster's body, protruding near the nape of his neck,
the wound where it entered rent and jagged by the resistance
of his weight before the blade snapped. He lay in shirt and
singlet and trousers, his discarded jacket and waistcoat tossed
carelessly down some distance away as if he'd been determined
not to risk a deflection of the weapon that killed him by a
button or the contents of his pockets.

Mole's awed voice, making a halting reconstruction, said,
"He must have taken the guard off the fire and put it back
again with the sword stuck through the grille – there's room for
the hilt in the bowl." He pointed to the red tape made redder
by the blood. "He tied it too – to make the point steadier and
the angle at which it reared correct – before he flung himself
on it." As if afraid the others wouldn't believe him, he asked,
"Well, how else could he have fixed it? Even in his state of
mind it's too much to ask that he should have tried to plunge
the blade into himself and it would have been awkward with
one so long if it had been possible at all." His brow wrinkled in
concentration: "As he fell on it the fireguard was pulled away,
but not cleanly. He toppled one way and the hilt was caught
in the grille and the sword sticking through him broke."

"You left this out," Cluff said, and bent to pick up the
button that had deadened the foil before Rigsby removed it.
"He forgot nothing."

Sickened, Barker turned away to the desk. He saw a sheet
of quarto paper on the writing pad and, after glancing at it,
thrust it blindly in the Sergeant's direction. "Nothing," he

repeated, looking at the uncased portable typewriter on its table at right-angles to the desk.

"'She wouldn't leave me alone,'" Cluff read, while Mole at his elbow checked him for accuracy. "'I wanted to finish with her but she demanded her price. I knew what it was doing to my wife and daughter and she held my future and theirs in the hollow of her hand. We arranged to meet at the hut, where we frequently met, and she was there first. I strangled her with a scarf and carried her up the ghyll to the pool. I forgot the scarf and left it in the hut. No one had a part in this but me, especially not Janet.'"

"I was right, after all," Mole said at length. "Of course I was right. She's only a girl. She wouldn't have had the strength."

CHAPTER XV

'Wait," Cluff said. "Wait!"

The nightman at the police station tried to read Rigsby's letter lying on the counter, upside down from his position behind it. The Duty Constable, in his helmet and greatcoat, who had been about to go off duty when they arrived, stopped halfway to the mouth of the corridor leading to the cells. "Don't fetch her for a moment," the Sergeant ordered, and swung round to the caretaker, brought with them from the school: "Where were you all day?"

"I'm off from twelve till four," Elijah whined. "They'd gone when I got back."

"And spend most of your time when you're there in the furnace room?"

"I do my job."

"Didn't you go up to his study?"

"I told you, I haven't got a key to his room."

"Into the corridor?"

"It's not my day. They empty their own baskets. I do upstairs and downstairs in the classrooms day and day about."

"You've never been much help since I've known you."

"I'd nothing to do with it, Mr Cluff."

"Go home!" the Sergeant said. "You're not even good for a statement." He collected the letter from the counter

and added, to the Duty Constable, "Now." Barker and Mole
and Clive followed him into the C.I.D. room and he went
behind his table but he didn't sit down, standing beside his
chair with his Burberry open and his hat pushed to the back
of his head. His attention was divided between the scarf Janet
had brought, still lying on the blotting-pad, and Rigsby's
suicide note, which he held in his hand. "It's typewritten," he
remarked.

"We know that," Mole thought and replied, aloud, "He'd
one in his office. Probably he always uses it."

"He was writing with a pen when I last saw him to speak
to." Cluff stared at the letter and then lifted his head: "I ought
to apologize?"

The Inspector made a valiant effort to conceal his
gratification: "The girl almost took me in too."

"But you were right about her reason. You said she was
protecting him."

"Haven't you emphasized their relationship?"

"It's not addressed: it isn't even signed," and the Sergeant's
eyes had gone back to the note.

"After all, he was locked in—"

The Sergeant started: "The key to the study! We should
have looked for the key."

"It was on the floor," Barker said. "Behind the door."

"It fell out of the keyhole," Mole suggested. "You weren't
gentle."

The Duty Constable guided Janet into the room, a hand
under her elbow, and to the chair in front of the table. He
settled her paternally and went back to the door but not
through it.

"He's dead," Cluff said, deciding to get it over with quickly. "Your father's dead." She drooped already with weariness and he allowed her to sob out her grief before he asked, "What point is there in it now?" as weary as she was. He handed her the letter: "He did it for you."

Their hearts went out to her and, "You can go," the Sergeant told her, turning on the Inspector, who had opened his mouth to protest: "Wouldn't I have tried to save him too if I'd been in her place? Is that a crime?"

"I wasn't going to say anything," Mole lied, and offered, "I'll take her home. No one's told her mother yet." He eased her to her feet and attempted to escort her to the door but she was staring at the scarf and ignored him.

"It's mine," she said, her mouth set stubbornly, and Barker wondered whether he'd really accepted her innocence. If she'd tried to protect her father, couldn't the reverse be true?

"Nothing can save his reputation," Cluff told her, "except allowing him credit for his sacrifice. If he killed her it was for you and he's paid his own debt but the whole story of his relationship with that woman has to come out. There has to be an inquest, two inquests. This is public property now." He watched her. "Perhaps I can keep you out of it personally, but not unless you're honest with me." He allowed her time to consider. "And there's your mother. Isn't she entitled to some of your affection too? Hasn't," and he used the past tense, "she been entitled to your affection?" He demanded, "Did you give it to her?" and his voice grew softer. "The past can be forgotten but there's still the future, and only the two of you to share it." He indicated the letter. "If you were guilty," he went on, "if everything you've told me is correct, no jury would convict with a defence lawyer putting that in front of it."

"It is mine," she insisted, looking at the scarf, in his hand now, and her eyes met the Sergeant's.

"I'm not disputing it."

She looked away and then surrendered. "I knew," she told them, "where he'd be. I didn't go home with my mother. I walked, in the town, on its outskirts, trying to make up my mind before I remembered my bicycle. When I went back for it I'm not sure what I was going to do. Perhaps I wanted to plead with them, both together, to end it: perhaps I hoped it wasn't really between them as I believed. I rode out and my father's car was parked where the track to the ghyll leaves the road, behind those cottages, out of sight, and so was hers. The track was too bumpy to ride on and I left the cycle nearby. I saw a light in the hut and I went round to the rear window. She was lying on the floor and my father was looking down at her, with the scarf in his hands."

"Your scarf!"

"I thought I'd lost it. Perhaps I left it in the dashboard compartment in our car." She wiped her eyes. "I saw him drop the scarf and he blew out the lamp but he lifted her up in the dark. He took her out and locked the door on to the verandah and I watched him struggle up the ghyll. I waited and waited and he came back but he didn't go into the hut."

"He saw your cycle," Mole said.

"But I'd left it in some trees off the track."

"What else could that final sentence of his note mean? It worried me a little," and the Inspector was speaking to Cluff. "Her father has been in his study all day. No one had told him she'd come here."

"Unless Lodge did," the Duty Constable interrupted.

"Lodge?" the Sergeant and the Inspector said together.

"He was here," the constable told them, "while you were talking to her in this room when she first came to the station. I was going to tell you – it didn't seem worthwhile. He was insisting, too, that she hadn't done it."

Janet continued, as if she hadn't heard them: "I'd brought the lamp from my cycle. I couldn't let the scarf stay there, in case anyone got into the hut and saw it. The window was open. I climbed in and got it and I had to come out the same way. The car hadn't gone when I got back but hers had and I had to wait again. My father came back a second time—"

"He'd been driving it down the road," Mole said.

"—and got in our car and went away. I rode home and he was standing by the garage when I got there."

"No wonder," the Sergeant said, "I saw you crying."

The Duty Constable staggered and a movement from the girl distracted Cluff: Clive came out from under the table: Mole and Barker were gazing at Lodge, who'd pushed the constable aside to get in. The Sergeant watched her shrink back, her fear tinged with contempt as the deputy headmaster dashed forward. "You're letting her go?" Lodge demanded, clutching at Mole, who was nearest to where he stopped, and, "I'll take you away from here," he pleaded with Janet.

"The Inspector will look after her," Cluff replied, and she was making for the door, by a roundabout route.

Mole collected his wits and he, too, set off for the outer office, into which the girl had vanished. Cluff's voice had a sharper edge to it: "Not you. Don't go!" Lodge, trapped between the table and the Duty Constable, who'd moved into the doorway after the Inspector's departure, halted, his eyes darting. "I'd have had to talk to you," the Sergeant said. "This is a good moment."

"The caretaker called on me a few minutes ago—"

"And you came straight here." He waited. "Again."

"It's terrible!"

"You knew she was going to take the blame on herself?"

"I was afraid so."

"You'd told Rigsby?"

"That you had her at the police station? Yes."

"And—?"

"He waited until after dinner and then he closed the school. I didn't see him any more."

"Or try to?"

"I'd nothing but disdain for him. I knew what was going on between him and Mrs Fairchild. He had his wife, and Janet."

"It didn't occur to you he might kill himself?"

"What am I supposed to feel?" Lodge's eyelids drooped. "It took me until almost three o'clock to clear the premises. Some of the children, those with both parents working, were slow in getting away."

"And then left?" Cluff asked, adding, when Lodge agreed, "Leaving him with the building to himself?"

"Until four, when the caretaker returns."

"Ample time for what he had to do. You'll have another chance to act as headmaster, as you did between Rigsby and his predecessor's death. Perhaps they'll be more careful about appointing a stranger now. Haven't you time to take a new wife if you're quick?"

"Is this all?"

"He left us a note," Cluff said, rising to his feet and going to the door, where he stood with his hand on the handle in an attitude of dismissal.

CHAPTER XVI

Barker, staring through the window into the dark, heard the Sergeant move in his chair and looked round to see him picking up his telephone. He dialled and said into the receiver:

"Dan?"

Chief Superintendent Patterson's voice came over the wire: "I didn't expect to hear from you."

"You waited in."

"One lives in hopes."

"You've read the papers?"

"More than that. I've quoted them to the Chief Constable, with a few additions I made up myself. About you. They had to be complimentary: I'd no option."

"Rigsby's dead."

"How?"

"In a locked room. Alone."

"You're satisfied?"

"I've been wallowing in a welter of confessions."

"Anything I can do?"

"No."

"I see," and after a pause Patterson asked, "Then why—?"

"I've been on the wrong track."

"But you've just told me—"

"It happened last autumn with Bright Culter."*

Another pause followed, then: "Whenever I hear from you I'm reminded of Annie's cooking."

"You're always welcome."

"You mean socially, of course," but the Superintendent's voice sounded more serious.

"I shan't rush over, Caleb."

"I'm getting old," Cluff said.

"Poppycock!"

"I think too much: it's time I retired."

"No doubt. A lot of people'll agree with you—"

"If you're going to take up that attitude," but the connection had broken and the Sergeant slammed down the receiver angrily. His bushy eyebrows lowered and almost met over the bridge of his nose. He glared at Barker: "What are you hanging on for?" and the detective-constable, unable to concoct a reply on the spur of the moment, mumbled inaudibly.

"All right!" Cluff said, and banged a clenched fist on the table top.

He paused for a moment in the outer office, glancing at the corridor leading to the cells as if he hadn't quite done with Fairchild, but dismissed whatever notion he'd had and made for the street. He told Barker, who was about to turn for his lodgings, "Come with me, then," and bulldozed through the town like a tank, setting a pace up the hill that would have done credit to a man twenty years younger. The stamp of their feet mingled with the panting of the dog and neither at the corner of Rigsby's avenue nor of Mole's did the Sergeant look sideways. The light in the cottage told Barker

<hr>

*   The Blindness of Sergeant Cluff

that Annie hadn't gone and she opened the door while they were still coming up the path. "You're sweating like a pig," she complained to Cluff. "What are you trying to do, have a seizure?"

He slapped his stick down and flung his hat and Burberry on their hooks and by the time Barker arrived in the living-room he was stuffing tobacco into his pipe, his face as black as thunder.

Annie made them a meal and stood over them while they ate. They moved to the fire with Jenet and Clive and before she left she looked in on them. "Don't let him sit up all night," she said to Barker. "He forgets what a bed's for."

Smoke curled from the pipe: the fire crackled: the clock ticked: the dog slept and so did the cat. In the end the Sergeant said, "So it's time I threw my hand in?" and Barker went on waiting, more and more certain he wasn't here for the sake of keeping Cluff company.

"She saw him," the Sergeant said, "carrying the body to the pool. She was there and he was there."

Barker murmured carefully, deliberately, "Her father killed himself."

"When I want your advice I'll ask for it."

The detective-constable turned out the lamp and cast a final glance at the fire before he followed Cluff into the passage and put on his own hat and coat. He stopped to hide the key of the front door under the flat stone in the flowerbed beside the porch and Clive joined him halfway down the garden path. They caught the Sergeant up as he opened a gate into a field where the lane ended and he made straight on, as the crow flies, for the moortop, then down the other side into the adjoining valley. They climbed the wall on to the road, not far from the lay-by with its snow plough and pile of chippings.

Cracknell answered their knock when they arrived at his door and told them, "She's out somewhere." They waited while he laced his boots and, near the hut, Cluff sent Clive ahead: "Find her for us!" The dog disappeared into the dark and the quiet was broken only by the noise of the waterfall.

"She hasn't been herself since that night," the forester said.

A shape moved down the ghyll towards them, after Clive, and she ran lightly, with hair floating, accompanied by a rustle of bracken, her feet seeming scarcely to touch the ground. "Abbie," Cluff said, holding out his hand. "It wasn't Janet Rigsby. You liked her but you couldn't be sure. I wasn't sure either, not until tonight. You saw them but the woman was dead and you didn't know who killed her. You didn't see that."

"I've never had a sister."

"She'd a father too, Abbie, but not like yours. And a mother. Gunnarshaw's not large but it's still a town. She's never learnt what you've learnt here."

"I'd have taught her."

"Were there so many others?"

"So many."

"Only to you. If you'd tried couldn't you have counted them on your fingers and still have had some to spare?"

"At night."

"I know. They disturbed you. They won't come back. She won't come back but she's safe. Her father's dead."

"It makes me happy."

"Was it like that either? Can't you tell me about it now?"

"A little man, last month—"

"Not Fairchild – about the night his wife died."

As she talked the possibilities grew for Barker and the facts began to fall into place, forming a new pattern. He heard Cluff say softly, "It's all yours, as it used to be, Abbie," and they left her in the hollow.

"It changed for her when they began to cut down the woods," Cracknell said at the bridge the tree-fellers had built, and they stopped there, contemplating the moors, the empty spaces about them giving an illusion of infinity to the land, though the unseen town lay only three miles down the valley. Barker imagined the smell of smoke but even when he saw the glow he hesitated to draw the attention of his companions to it. It grew pinker, reflected against the sky, spouting little tongues of flame: it waxed and waned and the sky turned darker again.

"There'd be some matches," Cluff said, "and I saw a can of kerosene by the stove."

A minute might have passed, or five, or perhaps half-an-hour. "There's no wind," and this time it was Cracknell speaking. "It won't spread."

"She'd take that into consideration when she set the hut on fire," the Sergeant replied.

CHAPTER XVII

"Twice," Cluff said. "I've been wrong twice."

"And this time?" Barker thought.

Once about Culter, once about Janet, and was it midnight, or after? There were no lights in the houses of the terrace and the night seemed so still that the detective-constable imagined he could hear the breathing of the people asleep behind the walls. He wished they'd never left the ghyll and his doubts had grown all the way along the road to Gunnarshaw until now he drowned in them. Twice already, and would a third time be the same? A dozen objections to the Sergeant's course of action dazzled him. Could they rely on the word of a half-mad girl, uncorroborated, and if they did, what indeed had she seen? Only a man in the night, as she'd seen Janet, as she'd seen her father, as she'd seen Fairchild once. If he'd been there at all was she capable of distinguishing one date from another in the confusion of her mind? What would people make of the ashes of the hut, that she'd deliberately destroyed, except a proof of her obsession to keep inviolate the countryside over which she roamed?

The Sergeant's arm lifted, its fist clenched to batter on the door, and Barker, without considering, grabbed and held it. "It's too uncertain," he said, and he could see Rigsby lying transfixed by the rapier in the pool of his blood, the agony of his dying imprinted on his features. The contents of the note he'd written, word for word, went round and round in his brain. "You can't ignore it," he begged, and if it wasn't true Rigsby couldn't speak for himself or deny it now. He pleaded, "Give it more thought. Nothing else can happen tonight. It might look different in daylight."

"This time," the Sergeant said, "I need to be right. There can't be any waiting."

"Lodge will never confess."

"So he's to get away with it?"

"Aren't you more important than he is?"

"Me?" and Cluff's surprise was genuine.

"To yourself."

"What kind of man would that make me?"

Could Barker still have stopped him, even now, if he'd begun to talk, about the Culter case, about Janet, about the dangers, evident and proven, of one man trying to step into another's skin, to think as he did and trace the springs of his actions? Could he have weakened further a confidence already shaken by past mistakes? Must he stand by and allow the Sergeant to make more errors, without lifting a finger to stop him? They weren't dealing with a moron but with an intelligent being, educated, and they couldn't go on sailing so close to the wind for ever. In the middle of the night, he thought, without authority, without evidence that would stand up in a court! If only Lodge wasn't in: if only he couldn't hear: if only he wouldn't come down – but if he didn't the Sergeant's knocking would waken the whole street, into a chaos of opening doors and windows, of shouted inquiries and demands for silence, with them at the centre of the vortex.

Tomorrow – and the word haunted Barker – tomorrow would have been time enough. They weren't any more sane tonight than Abbie. This wasn't proof but prejudice, foolishness not wisdom.

"Who's there?" a voice asked, deadened by the barrier of the door.

"Let us in!"

"What do you want?"

"It's Cluff. Do I have to ask you again?"

A chain rattled and a bolt shot back. A lock clicked and the Sergeant put a foot between the door and the jamb. He forced his way into the passage, lit by a low-powered bulb hanging in an opaque shade from the ceiling, and Barker stepped in as well, accompanied by Clive. Lodge, in a dressing-gown over pyjamas, with leather slippers on his feet, faced them, fumbling with the cord round his waist. Behind him, at the top of the stairs, his housekeeper, an old woman, grey hair dangling to her shoulders, the hem of her nightdress visible under an outdoor coat, clung to the banister, as pale as death, trembling.

"Where is it?" Cluff demanded, and none of them, Barker included, had the slightest idea to what he referred. Was there the least hint of fear in Lodge's eyes, the slightest of tensions stiffening his short body? The smile he forced looked wan and sickly.

The house smelt stale, with that curious smell, its components inseparable, often found in old houses with old people in charge, a miasma of existence within walls where fresh air was not allowed to penetrate, a little acrid, almost tangible, not wholly unpleasant. The aged housekeeper, installed since Mrs Lodge's death, looked as if she would faint at any moment and one of them ought to have gone to the foot of the stairs to catch her as she fell. It wouldn't be Cluff, or Lodge, and Barker wasn't able to get past to do it. The Sergeant's bulk blocked his way, swelling between the passage walls, and if he hadn't been tall himself it would have hidden Lodge from view.

"The key," Cluff said, and Lodge hunched, stepping back, his lips scarcely opening as he repeated, sibilantly, "Key?"

"You had one," Cluff stated, in a tone that brooked no contradiction. "The school's no more than six years old. No one's changed the locks on the doors since it was put up."

"Get out!" Lodge ordered. "Get out of my house!"

"Can you make me?"

"We've tolerated you too long in Gunnarshaw."

"Get dressed: you're coming with us."

"Show me why."

"You know."

"I've a right to."

"We'll discuss it at the station."

"I won't go!" but Lodge delayed a moment too long in his retreat and Cluff had him by the shoulder. "Clive!" Barker exclaimed, restraining the dog, and watched the Sergeant march the teacher up the stairs, past the housekeeper, still dumb, who lacked the power of movement except to press herself closer to the banister. Barker knotted one end of his handkerchief in Clive's collar and led him with the other. "Go back to bed," he advised as he went by the old woman in his turn.

"Is this where you were going to bring her?" the Sergeant

was asking as Barker arrived along the landing at the open door of a bedroom. "Or did you intend to move in with them? Which of them would you have married – the mother – or would you have had the courage to stake a husband's claim, not a father's, to the daughter?" Cluff stood over Lodge, whom he'd dropped on the edge of the bed, a harshness in his manner and an inflection in his tone he rarely employed, not the man at this moment Gunnarshaw knew. "You saddled a corpse with it," he accused, gratingly.

"I'll make you pay for this."

"Get his clothes," Cluff commanded, without turning his head.

Barker looked round the room and saw them on a chair. He did as he was told, handing underclothes and a shirt from its back, which the Sergeant took and hurled at his victim, sneering silently at Lodge's nakedness, the spindly legs bowed under the balloon of his belly, the narrow chest with a few curly hairs, the muscleless arms, the pale flesh coloured like the underside of a fish. He went through the pockets of the jacket and trousers before he passed them on and they were in it now, Barker thought, himself too, so what more was there to worry about?

The key-ring lay on Cluff's palm and he breathed more easily after Lodge, with the tails of his shirt flapping, had snatched at it and been thrust away. Light from the electric bulb sparkled on the two small brass keys and on the bright metal of lesser ones but the largest, black key was out of place, hardly the kind a man would carry about permanently in his pocket, certainly not in a bunch with his others. "You shouldn't have kept it," the Sergeant said. "You'd have inherited its twin, temporarily at least, and in any case it wouldn't have done to play the same trick twice." He detached it and put the others in the housekeeper's hand as they passed her again on the stairs: "I'll let you see him about the house but he won't be coming back." She still hadn't moved an inch or spoken a single syllable when they closed the front door as they went out.

The detective-constable, on one side of Lodge, had released the dog: Cluff walked on the other not caring whether it was night or day or who saw them, except that he would have to wait now, the hardest part. But the key he could feel at each step against his thigh, through the lining of his pocket, cheered him and he'd staked all he had on this, not his material possessions but what made him himself, his compassion, his feelings for others, his inner convictions. He felt like a man climbing the cliff of a sheer gorge, out of the blackness: he wasn't quite certain yet what he'd find when he got to the top but that he'd taken his decision at all to extricate himself made him happier.

The nightman on the counter goggled, startled out of his coma, and pinched himself to see if he was awake. "Lock him up," the Sergeant ordered, "and yourself with him. Stay with him and watch him."

The nightman's protests equalled Lodge's but Cluff cut one short with, "Barker'll look after the counter for you," and the other with, "Think it over for the rest of the night," before he went into the C.I.D. room with Clive.

It wasn't necessary, Barker thought, to have a man on duty during the small hours at all and the light behind the glass panel of the C.I.D. room door went out as he tried to settle down until dawn. It got colder in the office and his spirit sank to its lowest ebb, the longer the minutes the less his understanding of why they'd gone for Lodge so impetuously. Once during the night he tiptoed across the floor and opened Cluff's door a little way. In the light from the outer office he made out Cluff's form huddled in his chair on the other side of the table but he couldn't tell whether the Sergeant was asleep or awake. He heard Clive stir and pulled the door quietly to, unable so much as to doze himself. After some hours, when the outer office became intolerable, he made a journey down the corridor to the cells built on to the back of the station which, in its time, had been a private house. There were three of them but Mole used one as a store and another, where Fairchild slept peacefully, was rarely occupied. He looked through the peephole in the door of the third at Lodge lying fully dressed on his back on the bed, hands folded on his stomach, eyes wide open, the nightman, on a chair tipped against the wall, surveying him sulkily.

He delayed as long as he could when daylight came, because he couldn't see how much farther they were going to get now that the night had passed but finally he pulled up the blind, remembering a similar task in Fairchild's house, and switched off the lights. He kept expecting the C.I.D. room door to open but it didn't and they'd have to let Lodge go unless they made a charge against him. He went through the Criminal Code in his head and all the Regulations he could think of but he couldn't settle on anything that would give them the necessary excuse. He started to sweat a little and decided that if Cluff had to leave the force he was himself young enough to commence a new career.

The Duty Constable's long, low whistle took him by surprise and he wasn't in the mood for banter. He scorned as puerile the constable's, "What have you done, murdered the chap on nights?" and burst out, "We've got Lodge in the cells."

"You've got who?" Harry went through the manuscript books on the counter: "There's nothing in here about it," and swung round as Cluff and Clive came out of the Sergeant's room. "What is this place, a hotel?"

"Take over in the cell," Cluff told Barker. "Keep your eye on him. Harry'll send out for some breakfast."

"For Lodge too?"

"If he wants some."

"And you?" but Cluff and the dog were already leaving through the street door.

The town wasn't really awake as they made their way along its streets. A postman or two and a man delivering newspapers nodded at them: the rattle of milk bottles sounded here and there from side-streets. The Sergeant walked quickly, the school first on his list, and he thought grimly that soon it would have no teachers left. He supposed someone should warn whoever was next in seniority to Lodge or ring up the Divisional Education officer but he'd his own affairs to look after and they could attend to theirs.

The caretaker, subdued, opened the side entrance for him and he climbed the steps and prodded the policeman outside the broken door awake. The man said, "I thought the Inspector had forgotten me," and Cluff answered, "He probably has."

Except that they'd removed Rigsby the room was as he'd left it yesterday. They'd have taken photographs but he didn't want them and who, these days, left fingerprints that were relevant? A thought struck him and he looked at the typewriter, wondering whether a man could use the machine in gloves, but it was only a possibility to be kept in reserve. The key lay on the floor behind the door where Barker had said it was and it could have fallen from its lock but he didn't think that likely, though still, a lawyer with his wits about him would argue, if necessary, that Rigsby himself had dropped it. He picked it up by the ward and sealed it in an envelope he found in a drawer in the headmaster's desk. The key he'd taken from Lodge matched it exactly and the door lock wasn't badly broken: it fitted there too.

He looked at his watch. He didn't want to but it had to be done and they were up, as a matter of fact, when he arrived at the Rigsby house, if they'd been to bed at all. He went round to the back door and Mrs Rigsby let him into the kitchen, where Janet was sitting on a chair, gazing into the fire, the table set for a breakfast they hadn't eaten, bread on a board with a sharp knife to cut it, marmalade, crockery. Perhaps this final shock had numbed them or perhaps they realized, after thinking it over all night, that a solution, even of this sort, was preferable to the complications which they had dreaded for so long. Enough was enough and they couldn't have taken much more, either of them. Was it possible that in their innermost hearts they were glad of Rigsby's death? Didn't the daughter feel at last a misdirection in the love she'd lavished on her father, a vague knowledge that she'd been wasting her life by refusing to admit the truth of her adolescent yearnings? Was the mother relieved at the prospect of freedom from a husband who'd ceased to be a novelty long ago and proved only another man?

The questions he had to ask were easier to frame than he'd imagined and they might almost have been strangers to these happenings, uninvolved, discussing them loftily, as an academic exercise on the nature of humanity, whose faults they did not share. "I listened," he told the woman, "when I was here before, to what you said to Lodge and Janet listened on the landing." They didn't comment. "Your father," he said to the girl, and, "Your husband," to the mother. "I can clear him of some, at least, of the guilt. You needn't exist either with the belief that he was a murderer or that he was too weak to face the consequences of what had begun with Mrs Fairchild." He asked, "Will you grant him that?"

Mrs Rigsby looked at Janet, who looked back at her, and they were closer than they'd been that afternoon when he took tea with them at the school. Two in a house, he thought, is easier than three and allows of only one combination, nobody left out, no competition between one and another for the third, no division into opposing sides.

"We'll help you," Mrs Rigsby said.

"Then tell me about Lodge. When you came to Gunnarshaw it was only logical that your relationship would be intimate. You were strangers and he knew the school. For a while, at any rate, until he found his feet your husband would be dependent on him."

"I thought he was a lonely man. He'd lost his wife."

"Not a resentful one? He'd hoped to be appointed as headmaster and if he's ever held a post anywhere but here people have forgotten about it."

"He was eager to assist."

"You accepted him as a friend?"

"He was our first in this town, perhaps the only one my husband and I had in common. Our lives were separate, his at the school, mine in this house. Only Lodge visited us."

"Had you no friends either?" Cluff asked Janet.

"She had her father," Mrs Rigsby said. "He worshipped her when she was a child: she worshipped him."

"The child grew up."

"He saw that in the end. He was afraid of it. There was a gap in his life I'd grown too far from him to fill. Janet wasn't at his beck and call any more however much she wanted to be. He couldn't play with her as he had done or take her in his arms as he could a little girl."

"But Lodge kept coming?"

"My husband was often out. He interested himself in this activity and that, a committee here, a secretaryship there, a chairmanship, anything—. It didn't give him what he wanted and since last year he'd another reason for his absences." She watched her daughter. "Lodge came more frequently. I thought at first he came to see me, that we were sorry for each other, his life and mine both empty." She admitted, "I was tempted: we'd been thrown together," and said, "In the beginning perhaps it was that for him but I'm not young and I couldn't be moulded. It wasn't the love I could have given he was after and Janet was a woman too."

"Virgin," Cluff said to himself. "Unspoilt. Her body firm and untouched, an old man's Mecca."

"He tried to kiss me," Janet interrupted. "I was alone in the house. I saw his eyes: I felt him against me. His hands—"

"I'd been shopping," her mother added. "He didn't expect

me to come in."

"How long ago?"

"A few weeks."

"But you kept it from her father?"

"He'd been our friend. Could I ruin him for one moment of aberration?"

"Can you face the streets?"

"Must I pretend? My husband and I weren't in love. Running away isn't important to me."

"Then come to the police station." Janet moved as if she was going to get to her feet. "Only your mother," the Sergeant said. "It won't take long. You'll be all right in the house."

"I'll get my coat," Mrs Rigsby agreed.

"I've a call to make. Give me time. In twenty minutes or so."

He refused to think as he left the house any withdrawal now, any reconsideration, with Lodge in the cell and after the way he'd treated him, out of the question. He pulled his half-hunter from his waistcoat pocket to check the time and he still had Clive with him.

He hurried a little, to the High Street, and the citizens of Gunnarshaw had a set pattern in their lives, day in and day out, week in and week out, month after month, year after year. The manager of the bank, as he always did, crossed the road to the minute, from the usual direction, his approach unvarying, unbuttoning his coat to feel in his pocket for his keys. Cluff cut him off in the passage where the side door opened: "Lend me Will Stockwell for an hour or two."

"He's not in trouble?"

"Don't you know your staff – and me?"

"Yes. He'll go far."

"Farther because of what I want for him."

"No one else would listen to you, Caleb."

"We've had our lives."

"I'm one clerk short as it is. Shall I see Janet Rigsby back at all?"

"It's her life too."

"Give me credit for enough sense to see it's connected with that affair."

"I do."

"I didn't expect you to form a posse: I thought that went out with the Wild West." The manager smiled. "You've relied before on the fact that we went to school together."

"I shall again."

"My directors would be appalled."

"I won't tell them."

The manager unlocked the staff entrance to his bank and stepped aside to make way for his cashier. He looked down the passage and stayed with Cluff until Stockwell appeared: "The Sergeant wants you," and he left them together.

"There's nothing to be afraid of," Cluff said. "You're not ashamed to confess publicly you're in love with Janet Rigsby?"

"No."

"I'm not Cupid," and the Sergeant permitted himself a wry grin, "but she needs someone just now. If you haven't heard already you'll understand when you do." His eyes tracked up and down the youth's sturdy, thickset figure. "You play rugby," he said. "You're in Gunnarshaw's first team and you box as well, I think. You can look after yourself."

"If I have to."

"It shouldn't be too much for you."

He drew Stockwell after him, farther up the passage, and as
he talked he watched the young man's face, satisfied with what
he saw there, the mystification replaced by understanding,
then gratitude, finally by eagerness and resolution.

CHAPTER XVIII

"If that is a joke—!" and Inspector Mole fresh from the street, his expectation of a quiet day in his office shattered, couldn't find words to go on.

"I wish it was," the Duty Constable said.

The Inspector stuttered and he wasn't concerned personally but the vision he had of the probable consequences reduced him to a jelly. He managed, "The Sergeant's been going downhill for weeks. Has he had a breakdown? He can't be right in his head. Doesn't he realize – no charge, locked up in a cell? All night, you say! Patterson couldn't save him if he wanted to." He swung round and gaped at Mrs Rigsby, who'd come in behind him: "Good God!"

"The Sergeant asked me here."

"You!"

"I don't mind."

In the absence of a lead from the Inspector the Duty Constable came through the flap in his counter: "Will you wait in his room?" and he took her into Cluff's office, closing the door when he came out. "It mightn't be as bad as you think," he told Mole. "There's usually a method in the Sergeant's madness."

"I'll grant you," the Inspector replied, "he's had luck on his side up to now," and he ran a hand across his brow. "But it's hard on us. I'd be happier sitting on top of a volcano. 'It's a peaceful little place,' they told me when they gave me Gunnarshaw. 'Nothing ever happens there.'" He cleared his throat. "'Sergeant Cluff's got it all in hand,' they said. 'Crime doesn't exist.' I haven't had a quiet moment since I was posted."

He jerked nervously and leapt at Cluff, who entered the station too. Clive snarled but he paid no attention and his use of the Christian name showed his concern, "Caleb—"

"Is she here yet?" and when the constable nodded at the C.I.D. room Cluff added, "Good!"

"What's good about it? Lodge—" the Inspector began.

"Leave him to me," and the Sergeant pushed past him for the entrance to the corridor. The constable held Mole: "You'll have to. He's the C.I.D., not you," and they saw Clive sit down before Cluff turned a bend out of sight. The Inspector dusted his sleeve where the Duty Constable's hand had been: "Why doesn't he put the dog on the strength?"

"It won't let anything by if I'm any judge of what he told it," the constable said. "Us neither."

The Sergeant glanced at Fairchild's cell as he passed and the clerk was still asleep, making up perhaps for all the sleeplessness he'd endured during his years of matrimony. Before he went in to Lodge in the cell beyond he continued farther to an outer door, whose bolts he shot back. He looked briefly into the station yard, on one side of which a wooden palisade fenced off an area of waste land, once a garden now a wilderness, and pushed the door to.

He came back to Lodge's cell and called Barker out into

the corridor, ignoring the teacher's protests, and he left this door ajar. He asked, "How has he been?" in a low voice and the detective-constable, catching the inflection, whispered in reply, "It's hard to tell. He was still when I took over at first but then he got restless. He tried to talk."

"You didn't let him?"

"He soon shut up when I gave him no encouragement."

The Sergeant raised his voice: "I've got him now." Barker reached for the cell door to close it properly, only to find himself restrained, and in the same loud tone Cluff continued, "He hasn't a hope," and moved a little nearer to where they were both sure Lodge was listening.

"You didn't believe it," Cluff said, "even when Abbie Cracknell told us she'd seen him by the hut. A pity Fairchild's wife and Rigsby were so careful about going there independently in case anyone saw them leaving Gunnarshaw together. Lodge walked, of course, and arrived first. He'd have qualified as a burglar if he hadn't had ambitions as a murderer, not that the back window presented much difficulty only he couldn't refasten it when he left. He'd got the scarf Janet left once in Rigsby's car – at any time during the past weeks when it was parked at school or elsewhere – and he was waiting to strangle Mrs Fairchild with it. She was dead when Rigsby got there and the headmaster couldn't leave her in the hut – the least that would have occurred if he had would have been the publication of his liaison with her."

From time to time the Sergeant paused, as if Barker, in a gentler voice not carrying into Lodge's cell, had objected or interposed with views of his own.

"His motive?" Cluff continued. "In the plural. Number

one, he'd never forgiven Rigsby for being appointed to the position he ought to have had. Number two, he wanted Rigsby's daughter. If he couldn't turn the trouble he'd get the headmaster into to good effect in that respect by making Janet obliged to him he wasn't the man he thought he was. Did it even matter much if the murder wasn't actually proved against Rigsby? We'd pry once she was dead and his affair with Mrs Fairchild would be bound to come out. That ought to finish him at school and with his family too, leaving both ways open to Lodge."

He laughed: "But of course, he'd never a hope of the girl. An old fellow like that, and not even well preserved! I've just come from Rigsby's house: I've been talking to her. He lost his head once – she thinks he was trying to rape her. Fortunately, her mother arrived but he'd disgusted her once and for all. She wouldn't touch him with a barge-pole now."

He waited, to let this sink in. "He lived in hopes still, naturally. He stayed to watch what Rigsby did with the body and if Cracknell hadn't come across it Lodge would have brought it to our attention in some way. What he hadn't expected was Janet herself following her father and certainly not the confession she made when she believed him guilty.

"What's that you say – Rigsby killed himself and left that letter? Lodge had to convince us Janet was lying: he wouldn't have been much nearer with her in prison. I believed her myself and, if Mole didn't, we've never had much reason to rely on the Inspector's judgment. How am I going to prove what happened at the hut? I'm not." He wondered whether Lodge's heart leapt at this, whether hope sprang in him again. "Noble of her father," he said, "to do for Janet what she'd thought she was doing for him? You don't imagine he really killed himself? Lodge did that. He couldn't lose the girl: he couldn't give himself away: Rigsby wasn't getting into as much trouble as he'd hoped. He had to set the one free and rid himself of the other."

Cluff adopted a reasonable tone: "Would I have arrested him if I hadn't been relying on this second murder, when the evidence for the first is largely circumstantial? We found a study key in his house – it's one he kept from his own period of acting as head. I've been to the school to confirm that. By the way," and he pulled an envelope from his pocket and handed it over, "here's Rigsby's key. Lodge left it on the floor. Dust it for fingerprints."

He paused again, as if Barker was replying.

"Exactly. There should be some prints but if there aren't Lodge wiped it clean in order not to leave his own. How did he manage to fake the suicide? Simple. He knew when the caretaker was due and Elijah might be late but he'd never be early. Rigsby had closed the school. If Lodge had told him we'd got Janet wouldn't her father have come to us himself to make certain she was released? If he hadn't, does a man go to the trouble of uncasing his typewriter and typing a suicide note instead of using a pen that's to hand? Very well then, assume that Lodge wore gloves, he teaches chemistry, doesn't he? – a fact, incidentally, that puts poison out of the picture since it would have led us to him – he'd have some, rubber ones, thin enough to type in, but for a scientist he's not all that intelligent. If he remembered not to risk faking a signature and not to leave prints on the typewriter there'll be a sample of typescript done by Rigsby somewhere. We'll

compare it with the note, differences of pressure, of emphasis
– you know it'll speak for itself."

Barker didn't know anything of the kind and he doubted
whether Cluff did but he began to see the Sergeant's drift and
the means, maybe, justified the end.

"Science," Cluff insisted. "The science of forensic
medicine. He had to immobilize Rigsby before he killed him.
That bruise on the temple where he knocked the headmaster
unconscious before pushing him on to the sword – no doubt
he congratulated himself when he adjusted the body with its
head to the corner of the hearth as if it had hit the tiles in
falling. But there's the shape of the wound, the difference
between one hard object and another – child's play to an
expert like Doctor Hamm. Oh, Lodge has convicted himself
all right! I've probably missed something out, but haven't I said
sufficient, beginning with Abbie—? I forgot, his housekeeper
knows he was out on the night of Mrs Fairchild's death: he
cleaned his own boots and brushed the mud from the bottoms
of his trousers to hide the fact that he'd been walking on that
track but he didn't make a very good job of it."

"You've never mentioned it to her," Barker thought.

"I'll dig up something else," the Sergeant went on, in
pleased, confident tones. "Probably somebody saw him
apart from Abbie, that night or leaving the school yesterday
afternoon, later than he said he did. It's not necessary but
I'm in no mood to miss anything." He stopped talking and
listened. "Who's that? In the office. Come along – you've got
a job on that key."

Barker opened his mouth to say, "The door?" and Cluff
shook his head violently, dragging him bodily along the

corridor, putting his own feet down heavily on the concrete floor. They picked up Clive at his guardpost and the Sergeant halted in the entrance to the outer office, surprised because he'd expected only Mole and the Duty Constable there. He growled a little and muttered at Patterson, "I thought you weren't going to rush over from Headquarters."

The Chief Superintendent, his expression worried, said, "I wasn't," and glanced at a man with him. "Mr Foley rang me up."

Cluff glared at the solicitor: "Couldn't you have come to me?"

"After what I'd heard it wouldn't have been much use."

"The housekeeper got in touch with you?"

"Luckily she'd that much sense. It's not only the arrest, the lack of a charge, it's the manner of doing it—"

"You're not a Gunnarshaw man," the Sergeant said. "Did the housekeeper try you first or wouldn't any of the older firms listen to her?"

"I'm making an application to the court—"

"Apply away!"

Patterson's unease increased: "Caleb—"

"You're on his side?"

"I demand to see Lodge," Foley said.

Patterson advised, "You'll have to allow that," and Mole joined in, "He's got the law to back him up."

The Sergeant planted himself more firmly in the mouth of the corridor and if it came to a battle, the Duty Constable thought, where would he come in? He didn't like the expression on Cluff's face and the trapped look in his eyes, his sudden weariness.

The solicitor braced himself and started forward. Inspector Mole danced a jig in his excitement: the Chief Superintendent began to move in Foley's wake: the Duty Constable remembered his pension with regret because of the demands friendship imposed on him: Clive bared his teeth and growled: the door of the C.I.D. room opened and Mrs Rigsby stood on its threshold.

Behind Cluff, Barker turned suddenly and ran back along the corridor, pursued by the Sergeant's orders to stop. He disappeared round its corner and Cluff faced his tormentors. "If you'd given him time," he said, "if you'd given me time. All I wanted was a little time."

Barker reappeared, shouting: "He's gone," and skidded to a halt, though only for a moment. "The yard door's open. I'll go that way—"

"Barker!" and this time the Sergeant's tone allowed of no disobedience. His weariness had gone as quickly as it had appeared and he set off across the office for the street door, at a run, Clive bounding ahead of him, leaving the others with their mouths gaping. He pushed the solicitor out of his way: "Now do something for him," and at the door he very nearly knocked Doctor Hamm, coming in as he was going out, sprawling. The doctor swore but he'd no opportunity to complain because Cluff and the dog had vanished. He turned to the people in the office, who hadn't moved, and looked at them quizzically. "So," he said, with a wealth of meaning, "I'm to be squashed flat for my pains, am I? I came to lend a helping hand – much thanks I get for it. There's something about that bruise on Rigsby's temple that doesn't satisfy me—"

He didn't get any further because Barker erupted from the

mouth of the corridor and he had to take rapid avoiding action to escape a second time the damage he'd only just risked from Cluff.

CHAPTER XIX

J anet stood with the table between them and he'd been so changed when he burst in through the kitchen door she'd hardly recognized him. The knot of his tie had slipped and his collar had come adrift from his front stud as if he'd been clawing at his neck. His face had turned a deep purple in colour and he breathed through his mouth and not through his nose, gulping in great draughts of air. It wasn't that his suit was ragged but, crumpled and creased, she knew that he'd slept in it. His shoes were muddy, with bits of grass caught in the welts.

She wasn't afraid of him at first and wondered how she'd ever been afraid of him, and that she was alone in the house didn't disturb her. Had she expected him since the Sergeant had visited them earlier? It didn't occur to her to ask where he came from because Cluff hadn't mentioned his arrest and she waited for him to speak but for a long time he couldn't. When he did he repeated her name, over and over again, and, though his distress was obvious and shocking, she felt for him only loathing. His limbs trembled and he kept casting backward glances at the door, a hunted creature, but vermin for which she had no pity.

"Hide me," he pleaded, and her lips curled.

He began to sidle towards her and her heart missed a beat

but recovered. He said, "I did it for you. I did it all for you."

She couldn't understand and he was coming nearer, making her less sure of herself, as she'd been that day in the living-room when he'd groped for her, his mouth hanging loose, a trace of saliva at its corners. His breath came more easily and he added, "I killed her for your sake. I wasn't to know you'd go after your father."

A coldness stabbed at her and she fell back, a little closer to the wall. His voice went on: "But I saved you, when Cluff would have put you on trial, when you'd have gone to prison. I saved you! I got you away from him. It's me you owe it to."

"Not you?" but her voice sounded low and unsteady in her ears. "He can't harm me," she thought. "He won't! And I wasn't afraid of him. I wasn't! I'm as strong as he is. I can protect myself if I have to." But he was changing again, not back to the Lodge she'd known, hard this time and cruel, his pupils contracting, very bright, a madness in his face.

"Hide me," he repeated. "What was your father to you?"

"No," she said, "no," not denying his request but trying to rebut a growing suspicion that deprived her of movement.

"In the attic, in the underdrawing – only until dark. They'll be looking for me. Until I can give them the slip. Your mother won't mind. I've done her a favour. I've done you one. You loved him and he left you for a woman like that. Aren't you glad I killed him too—?"

She groaned and fear was suddenly real, flooding over her in a great wave. He said, "If only I could kill Cluff as well. Without him we wouldn't have been found out, we could have been together—"

"We!"

Did her face betray something of what she felt, or was it implicit in that single syllable? His eyes narrowed and his glance was sharp, pregnant with a doubt that he strove to reject. His lips widened in a smile, the idea unthinkable, and he was himself, Lodge, with blood on his hands, and invincible. He's escaped from the police station and he'd escape from the town, from the country, not alone, taking her with him.

He'd forgotten her mother and he couldn't remember how it had begun, with the death of his own wife perhaps, with Rigsby's appointment to the post he'd counted on, his envy, his resentment, the Janus face he'd had to show to the world, his pride in the smiling villain he was. All that was behind him, unworthy, an empty dream, a mirage. She was here and he'd aimed at her, nothing else important, the taste of her lips, the smooth skin under his fingertips, the soft hair, the yielding globes of her breasts, the delights she hid not from him but from the world so that she could reveal them only to him, reaching for him, engulfing him, joining him to her. "Love me," he said, and held out his arms, willing her to come to him.

Who was this? Not Janet. Would Janet have looked like that? Would Janet have refused him as this impostor was doing, someone in Janet's shape, adopting her form, trespassing in that body which was his? His head craned forward on his neck: his sight blurred, making her outlines waver, and this one had stolen her from him. Was that his hand, crawling like a snake on the surface of the table to the knife lying beside the loaf on the breadboard? Whose scream was that? Not Janet's. He loved Janet. Janet would hide him. But this girl would hand him over without a qualm. Janet would love him and the stranger cringing in front of him would give herself to anyone, but not to him.

The knife in his hand flew across the room. An intolerable weight descended on his back, hurling him to the floor, driving the breath out of his chest. He twisted and writhed in an ecstasy of effort and this incubus held him fast. She was screaming and screaming and screaming and however she screamed he couldn't get to her. "Janet! Janet! Janet!"

Not flesh but fur. Not blows but teeth. Cluff was dragging the dog away and lifting Stockwell, calming him. "It's all right," he said, and the youth's sanity was slow in returning. "She's all right," and Stockwell shook himself, stumbling to the girl, quiet now but trembling, her knees sagging. "All right. All right," the Sergeant said, bent to hold the dog, and she swayed into Stockwell's arms. Over her shoulder as he held her with her head buried against him, hugging her tightly to lessen the shudders that tore through her, his eyes reminded Cluff of Clive's eyes, an adoration in them, an inexpressible respect and thankfulness. Lodge, on his knees on the floor, leaning on his hands, his head hanging, was an animal too, but one to be destroyed, rabid, uncontrollably wild.

Then they were all there, Barker, Mole, the Chief Superintendent, Hamm, the Duty Constable, the solicitor, Foley, her mother, who went to her and accepted without objection Stockwell's refusal to surrender her.

"He killed them both," the girl said at last, but she lifted only her head from her sanctuary and clung to the youth. "He told me so."

"Will you defend him now?" the Sergeant asked the solicitor, and Foley shook his head slowly, his eyes on that babbling wreck of a man, straying from Lodge to the bright-bladed knife.

"Take him," the Sergeant said, and Lodge didn't understand because nothing existed for him any more. Mole on one side and the Duty Constable on the other escorted him out of the house, down the drive to the waiting cars, round which a small crowd of neighbours had gathered.

"I could have saved myself the trouble," Hamm said. "You knew already what I came to the station to tell you," and a broad grin lit up Cluff's face. He herded them out in their turn and said from the doorway, to Stockwell, "I promised you'd be back at the bank. Don't overdo it. There's a lifetime ahead for you both."

Mrs Rigsby's eyes met his and she smiled too.

They made themselves comfortable, Cluff and Patterson in the armchairs, Barker on the couch, and Annie Croft moved briskly, clearing away the crockery they'd used for their meal. When she brought them their cups of tea the Chief Superintendent almost expected her to burst into song. Before she left them for her kitchen she handed the Sergeant his pipe and tobacco and put a box of matches on the arm of his chair. Jenet slept on his knees: Clive, on the rug, leaned his head on the fender.

"Now you can tell him," Cluff said. He watched the smoke curl from his pipe, blue and lazy, while Barker went over what he'd been told in the police station corridor outside Lodge's cell, omitting nothing.

The Superintendent considered for a long time before he said, "Where did you get those details from? You're becoming able in your old age." He paused. "The world's upside down. Anyone with less respect for science than you in our job I've never met."

"Could I have proved it?"

"Perhaps," and Patterson grinned. "I don't know."

"How else to get over Rigsby's note?"

"You're an old fox—"

"And it wasn't worth the trouble. I'd have been hours in the witness box."

"A blessing for the judge you won't be. For counsel as well." The Superintendent sipped his tea. "All of it was deliberate, of course."

"Did I make it up?"

"You wouldn't have hesitated if you'd had to. And he was meant to escape."

"I hoped he'd make a break for it. That's why I treated him as I did."

"And knew where he'd go. You'd got her mother out of the way."

"There wasn't any other place. I'd Stockwell instructed and on guard."

"It didn't satisfy you merely to find a solution?"

"Janet needed a solution too."

The Superintendent got to his feet: "It's time I was going." His voice sounded regretful. "I've got a feeling I shan't be wanted in Gunnarshaw in a hurry again, whatever happens." He stopped in the middle of the room. "Did you mention retiring when you talked to me on the phone?"

The Sergeant put the cat down and got up too.

"I'll wait," Patterson said, "if you'd like to draft out your resignation."

"Take us in to the station," the Sergeant replied. "It's on your way."

"You're not going to write a report?" Patterson exclaimed, in mock astonishment.

"I want a word with Fairchild."

"I'd forgotten him."

"If I can get him to go about it properly it mightn't be so bad for him. He's a houseful of stuff to make some restitution with."

"I'll come to the auction," the Chief Superintendent promised. "I've a wife to keep sweet as well."

Barker helped the Sergeant into his Burberry and Clive preceded them down the garden path to Patterson's car in the lane. Annie Croft watched them from the porch.

"You know," Cluff said, with one foot in the car and one foot out of it, "when Fairchild's released from prison I'd like him to meet Abbie Cracknell."

"You won't be at a loss for a job when you do go," Patterson replied.

"How's that?" and Cluff sounded suspicious.

"Why not start a marriage bureau?" Chief Superintendent Patterson asked. "You can't deny you're getting plenty of practice in."

The next Cluff…

Coming soon

Sergeant Cluff and the Price of Pity

by the same author

Published by The British Library

SERGEANT CLUFF STANDS FIRM
THE METHODS OF SERGEANT CLUFF

Published by Great Northern Books

SERGEANT CLUFF GOES FISHING
MORE DEATHS FOR SERGEANT CLUFF
THE BLINDNESS OF SERGEANT CLUFF

www.gnbooks.co.uk